THE LEGO BATMAN MOVIE

BUILD YOUR OWN STORY
ROGUE CITY

by
Tracey West
Based on the story by
Seth Grahame-Smith
and the screenplay by Seth Grahame-Smith
and Chris McKenna & Erik Sommers
and Jared Stern & John Whittington,
based on LEGO Construction Toys.

■SCHOLASTIC

Scholastic Children's Books

Euston House,

24 Eversholt Street,
London NW1 1DB, UK

A division of Scholastic Ltd
London ~ New York ~ Toronto ~ Sydney ~ Auckland
Mexico City ~ New Delhi ~ Hong Kong

This book was first published in the US in 2017 by Scholastic Inc.
Published in the UK by Scholastic Ltd, 2017

ISBN 978 1407 17733 5

Based on the story by Seth Grahame-Smith and the screenplay by Seth Grahame-
Smith and Chris McKenna & Erik Sommers and Jared Stern & John Whittington.

Printed and bound by CPI Group (UK) Ltd, Croydon, CR0 4YY

2 4 6 8 10 9 7 5 3 1

www.scholastic.co.uk

BUILD YOUR OWN STORY

This book isn't like other books. It tells the story of Batman and his quest to save Gotham City from the Joker and his Rogues, but it doesn't have a beginning, a middle and an end.

It has one beginning, lots of middles and even more endings.

How does that work? That's where you come in. As you read each piece of the story, you'll be given a choice about what Batman does next. You'll keep making choices until you build one story all the way to the end. When you're done, you can go back to the beginning and start building a whole new story!

There are many possible endings, but there is one best ending possible: for Batman to defeat the Joker and end up with Batgirl, Robin and Alfred on his team. When you see the Bat-Signal you'll know you've found the best ending of all!

GOT IT? GREAT! NOW GET READY TO BUILD!

Gotham City was in a panic, and, as usual, the super-villains were to blame.

The Joker, that green-haired, white-faced baddie with a twisted sense of humour, had masterminded the plan. He had one goal: to take over Gotham City.

The first part of the plan took place in the air. The Joker and some Rogues hijacked an aircraft with a powerful payload: eleven million sticks of dynamite.

Phase two took place on the ground at the Gotham City Energy Plant. The super-villain known as the Scarecrow used his toxic fear gas to get past the security guard. Other evil-doers followed him onto the power plant grounds:

Harley Quinn, the gymnastic jester;

The Riddler, a masked puzzle fiend;

The Penguin, a tuxedo-wearing troublemaker;

Killer Croc, the super-strong reptilian wrestler;

Clayface, the powerful, monstrous mud man;

Egghead, the evil scientist with the enormous brain;

Two-Face, the crime boss with the split personality;

Captain Boomerang, the bad guy with exploding boomerangs (what else?);

Bane, the mightily muscled masked wrestler; and

Catwoman, the master thief with mad skills.

These Rogues, and a bunch of others, stormed the power plant and took over the Core Containment Room. The Joker brought the plane and its explosive cargo to the energy plant. The Penguin's pet penguin minions waddled towards it and started to drill into the core so the Rogues could attach the bomb. Then the Joker gave Commissioner Jim Gordon a call.

"Listen up," the Joker said. "At this very minute a Joker Bomb – that's trademarked – is being attached to the inside of the main energy core."

Citizens of Gotham City gathered around their TV sets, anxious to learn what the Joker would do next.

"If the mayor isn't here in five minutes to

negotiate the city's surrender, then we'll blow up the energy core!" the Joker exclaimed.

The frightened citizens gasped. If the Joker blew up the energy core, Gotham City would lose all power!

"The shock wave will hit Gotham City," the Joker threatened. "And you wouldn't want that, would you? Now give me the mayor! Joker out."

Inside Gotham City police headquarters, Commissioner Gordon turned to the mayor. "Madam Mayor, I cannot ask you to do this," he said.

"Jim, did you find Batman?" she asked.

"No, ma'am," Gordon admitted.

"Then we have no choice," she said. "The Joker has the upper hand. We have to surrender Gotham City. I'm sorry."

She climbed into a police helicopter, and it flew off. Over at the energy plant, the Joker grinned when the helicopter arrived, hovering overhead.

A voice crackled from the helicopter sound system. "Lowering mayor package through the hole."

Police lowered the mayor through the hole that

the Joker had blasted into the energy core. She stared at the ground.

"I've got only one thing to say to you, Joker," she said, her voice muffled. "Do you ever play roulette?"

"On occasion," the Joker replied.

"Well, let me give you some advice," the mayor said.

The Joker grinned, amused. "I'm all ears."

"When playing roulette … always choose black!"

Swoosh! Batman had been hiding in the helicopter! He jumped out from behind the mayor, swooping down to confront the Joker.

"Batman!" the Joker cried. "What are you doing? You're completely outnumbered here. Are you nuts?"

"You wanna get nuts?" Batman yelled. "Come on, let's get nuts!"

"Get him!" the Joker yelled to the Rogues.

The super-villains charged at Batman.

Bam! Pow! Crash!

Batman battled them all. He kicked, he punched, he busted out awesome karate moves. He sent batarangs zipping through the air. One by one he took down the evildoers until only one was left … the Joker!

The Joker floated away from the energy core in a hot-air balloon. Batman leaped up and grabbed the Joker's hand.

"I got you," Batman told him.

"Oh yeah?" the Joker asked. "Well, there's only one problem: who's gonna defuse the bomb?"

Batman looked down. The Joker Bomb – dynamite, curly wires and a big, red ticker – was attached to the energy core. The timer was ticking down. Batman had only seconds to deactivate it.

"It's gotta be one or the other, Batman," the Joker pointed out triumphantly. "Save the city or catch your greatest enemy. You can't do both."

IF BATMAN TAKES THE BAIT AND TRIES TO CATCH THE JOKER, GO TO PAGE 39.

IF BATMAN DECIDES TO SAVE THE CITY, GO TO PAGE 99.

CONTINUED FROM PAGE 152.

"It's weed-whacking time," Batman said.

He sliced through one of the thick vines with his batarang. The broken piece of vine fell to the ground.

Batman looked at Barbara. "Told ya."

Then something strange happened. Three more tendrils of the vine started growing from where he had just cut!

"Batman, look!" Barbara cried. "When you cut one vine, three more grow back!"

The three vines wrapped around Batman and Barbara. Batman frantically slashed at them.

"Just. Stop. Growing!" Batman cried in frustration.

The vines wrapped around Batman and Barbara like a thick cage. Batman couldn't move his arms or legs. He heard Poison Ivy laugh.

"Now you're trapped in a plant prison!" she said.

Then he heard Barbara Gordon through the vines.

"I told you so!"

THE END

CONTINUED FROM PAGE 90.

Superman picked up Batman under one arm.

"Hey!" Batman protested.

Superman ignored him and flew up to a window on the third floor of City Hall. Then he hovered there.

"Check it out, Batman!" he said. "Joker's got a crowd in there. I can hear them with my super-hearing."

Batman produced a suction-cup device from his Utility Belt and stuck it to the window. "I can hear them too."

Killer Croc was complaining to the Joker.

"I hate being in charge of the aquarium," he growled. "Everyone thinks I'm one of the attractions. They keep asking to take selfies with me."

Catwoman stepped up. "Being in charge of animal control is *purrrr*-fectly boring. Where are the diamonds? Where are the *puurrrr*-ls?"

The Joker swung around in his desk chair. "Complaints! Complaints! Complaints!" he exclaimed. "That's all I've heard ever since I've become mayor of Gotham City. What a thankless job!"

"I'll thank ya, Mayor J," Harley Quinn said. "I think you're doing a great job."

"Of course I am, but it's no fun!" the Joker complained. "I wish I could blast this whole city into the Phantom Zone!"

"Well, why don't cha, baby?" Harley asked. "The Justice League is busy running all over Gotham right now. We can just go to Superman's Fortress of Solitude and grab the Phantom Zone Projector."

The Joker grinned. "Why yes, we can!"

"Oh no, you can't!"

Superman flew through the window, breaking it. Batman dropped to the floor.

"Superman! Batman! You don't have an appointment with Mayor J," Harley Quinn informed them.

The Joker's goons converged on Batman and Superman.

Pow! Bam! Wham! Batman dropped each thug that came after him.

"Justice doesn't need an appointment," Batman said.

"Game's over, Joker," Superman said. "We're taking back Gotham City."

The Joker stood up. "Oh, is that so?"

He picked up a drink can and shook it. Then he aimed it at Superman. A glowing green rope snaked out and wrapped around him.

"It's … Kryptonite," Superman said, struggling to break free.

Batman was still punching the Joker's goons. Before he could break away, three of them picked up Superman and carried him away.

"Sorry to run, Batman," the Joker said. "But I've got a Phantom Zone Projector to steal."

He raced out of the office. Harley Quinn followed him. "Right behind you, Mayor J!"

IF BATMAN RUSHES OFF TO HELP SUPERMAN, GO TO PAGE 69.

IF BATMAN CHASES AFTER THE JOKER, GO TO PAGE 143.

CONTINUED FROM PAGE 123.

"I think it means something that the word 'Grant' is capitalized," Batman said. "The Riddler must be sending us to Grant Park. It's only open during the day, like the riddle says."

"Glad you figured that out all by yourself," Barbara said dryly.

They hopped in the Batmobile and headed to Grant Park, an oasis of trees in the middle of the crowded city. Batman jumped out of his Batmobile.

"All right, Riddler! Show yourself!" he called out.

He got no response. The only sound was birds chirping in the trees.

Then Batman heard a buzzing sound. The question mark-covered drone was flying towards him again. It stopped in front of him and dropped another note.

Good work, Batman!
You've guessed my first riddle correctly.
But you didn't think finding me would be easy, did you?
Now riddle me this:

Moss only grows on this side of a tree.
Go twenty blocks this way and that's
where I'll be.

"Since when does moss grow on trees?"
Batman asked.

IF BATMAN AND BARBARA GO
NORTH, GO TO PAGE 24.

IF BATMAN AND
BARBARA GO SOUTH,
GO TO PAGE 147.

CONTINUED FROM PAGE 158.

Batman pulled the wire from the red port. Sparks shot from the machine. Then he saw sparks shooting from Barbara's metal beanie that was protecting her from the Mind Control Machine.

"Our beanies are fried!" Barbara cried. "We've got to get out of here, or we won't be protected from—"

You will do as I say.

Batman heard Scarecrow's voice inside in his head.

All residents of Arkham Asylum, return to your cells!

The waves from Scarecrow's Mind Control Machine had hit them! Batman couldn't fight it. He could see that Barbara couldn't fight it, either.

"Yes, Scarecrow," they both said.

Then they marched off to their cells in a daze...

THE END

CONTINUED FROM PAGE 171.

"Surrender? No way," Batman said. "We're going to rescue Superman and take back this city."

"And I can help you," Catwoman said.

Batman stared at her.

"She might be useful," Alfred said. "Getting into Gotham City Hall has been difficult."

"Fine," Batman said. He unlocked her cuffs. "Let's go."

They squeezed into the Batmobile and sped towards City Hall. Along the way, they formulated a plan...

A few minutes later, Catwoman walked up the steps to City Hall, flanked by two thugs dressed in black. Their faces were covered by cat masks.

The two guards at the door stopped her.

"What's your business with Mayor Joker?" one of them barked.

"I just want to congratulate him, of course," Catwoman said. "It's not every day a super-villain captures one of the greatest Super Heroes of all time."

One of the guys in the cat masks coughed loudly.

"That's right, Superman is one of the greatest heroes of all time, and the Joker has caught him," Catwoman went on. "And I just want to pay my respects."

The guards stepped aside, and Catwoman and her thugs walked through. They marched into the mayor's office. The Joker sat at his desk, flanked by six of his goons. Behind him stood Superman, wrapped in Kryptonite chains. His eyes were closed.

The Joker stood up from his desk, grinning. "Catwoman! Have you come to congratulate me?"

"Of course, Joker," Catwoman replied. "Capturing Superman is *purr*-fectly fabulous."

"Now all I have to do is capture Batman," the Joker said. "Then I can sit back and enjoy being mayor."

"The only place you'll be sitting in is prison," said one of the thugs, taking off his cat mask. He was wearing the batmask underneath.

"Batman!" the Joker exclaimed.

"Fun's over, Joker," Batman said. "We are taking back Gotham City."

The other thug took off his cat mask.

"What's Bruce Wayne's butler doing here?" the Joker asked.

"That's not important," Batman replied. Then … *Pow!* He slammed the Joker with a powerful punch.

The Joker's thugs charged at Batman, Catwoman and Alfred, but they were no match for the trio.

Bam! Blam! Wham! Batman, Catwoman and Alfred took them down one by one with serious martial arts moves. When the last thug fell, Batman ran over to Superman and unwrapped the kryptonite chains.

Superman's eyes fluttered open. "Batman? Thanks for saving me!"

"I had some help," Batman admitted. "From Bruce Wayne's butler and Catwoman…"

He turned his head. Catwoman was gone. But she had kept her promise.

"It's too bad that she likes being a villain," Alfred remarked. "You two would make a great team!"

THE END

CONTINUED FROM PAGE 168.

A metal arm extended from the Bat-Sub. It turned the smaller gear.

Whoosh! The tube opened, and Alfred got sucked inside it! He was propelled to the surface of the water.

Batman pulled a lever on the Bat-Sub, and the craft shot like a rocket up through the water. When it reached the surface, Batman opened the cockpit and pulled Alfred inside the sub.

"Thank you, Master Bruce," Alfred said, when Batman pulled the gag off him.

"No problem," Batman said. "Now let's get you home."

The Bat-Sub descended into the water again, this time swiftly travelling forwards through the reservoir. It entered an underwater channel that ended at a dock underground in a rocky cave.

Batman climbed out of the sub. "Alfred, I could go for some pizza bites," he said. "Not the pepperoni ones, though. They're—"

"Batman! Is this your secret hideout?"

Barbara Gordon had climbed out of the sub. She was still wearing her official Bat gear.

"You're still here?" Batman asked.

"I was going to ask you about that, sir," Alfred said. "She appears to be, well, part of our team."

"Well, kinda sorta," Batman replied.

Barbara was looking around. "Cool cave," she said.

"No," Batman said. "*This* is a cool cave."

He pressed a button on the rocky wall, and a secret door opened up into the Batcave. Lights from the high-tech equipment glittered against the smooth, sleek black floor and walls.

Barbara looked around in wonder. "Yeah, you're right. *This* is cool."

One of the large screens flickered on to show a news anchor standing in front of Gotham City Hall.

"Breaking news," she said. "Gotham City has been saved!"

"No, it hasn't," Batman said.

"The Justice League has saved the day. They captured the Joker and his Rogues, and have restored the mayor to City Hall," the reporter went on.

The camera turned to Superman.

"Just doing my duty as a Super Hero," he said with a dazzling smile.

Batman picked up a remote and shut off the feed.

"That's great news, isn't it, Batman?" Barbara asked.

"Yeah, great," Batman mumbled. But he didn't mean it.

I like saving Gotham on my own! he thought.

THE END

CONTINUED FROM PAGE 16 AND 88.

Batman and Barbara travelled twenty blocks north of the park – and found themselves in front of the Gotham City Orphanage.

"Uh-oh," Barbara said. "I hope the Riddler isn't giving these orphans any trouble."

They got out of the Batmobile. A bunch of orphan boys and girls ran towards them. One of the boys had been hanging upside down from a tree branch when Batman pulled up. He did a triple-back somersault off the tree and landed perfectly on the grass. Then he cartwheeled across the lawn to see Batman.

"Hey!" Batman growled. "This is official Super Hero business. Has anyone seen the Riddler?"

The kids shook their heads. Just then, the drone appeared.

"Not again," Batman grumbled. The drone dropped another riddle in front of him.

Not done yet, Batman!
  Riddle me this:
  What is holy but doesn't have any holes?

Batman frowned and crumpled up the note. "I'm sick of this wild goose chase. I'm done chasing the Riddler."

"Holy without holes – that must be a church!" piped up the acrobatic boy. "I bet the Riddler is in Cathedral Square."

"Of course!" Barbara said. "What's your name, kid?"

The boy grinned. "Dick Grayson, orphan, at your service."

"Let's keep looking," Barbara urged Batman. "We can bring Dick with us. He's clever."

"There's not enough room in the Batmobile," Batman said, but Dick was already whooping with joy.

"Hooray! Let me go and get a permission slip!" Dick cried.

He raced off and returned shortly after with a piece of paper. "The director of the orphanage says it's okay if I go with you on official business." He turned and waved to the other orphans. "Can you believe it? I get to hang out with Batman."

"Let's go," Batman said. "We're going to get the Riddler, and then I'm bringing you *both* back here."

He drove to Cathedral Square – but the Riddler wasn't waiting for them. Instead, the drone flew up again with another riddle.

Amuse me, Batman.
Park your Batmobile here,
And you will find me.
Riddler
Out!

"This is an easy one," Batman said. "Amuse. Park. He's at the amusement park."

"What do you think, Dick?" Barbara asked the boy.

"Well, if you look at the first letter of each line, it spells something," Dick replied.

IF THEY GO TO APARO PARK NEXT, GO TO PAGE 46.

IF THEY GO TO THE AMUSEMENT PARK NEXT, GO TO PAGE 73.

CONTINUED FROM PAGE 103.

Batman pointed to a watch on his wrist. "See that counter?" he asked, and Robin nodded.

He clicked a button and figures appeared:

Batman: 5,678,483

Everyone else: 0

"These are all good ideas Batman has had, and this is everyone else," he said. "So we're doing this projector thing."

Batman called for his Batwing. He, Dick and Harley Quinn flew to Superman's Fortress of Solitude in the frozen north.

"Harley, you stay here," Batman said. "Kid, I'll keep Superman busy while you sneak into that vent and get the projector. Got it?"

He pointed to a very narrow vent leading into the walls of ice.

"Copy that," Dick said eagerly. He squeezed into the vent.

Batman walked up to the door of the Fortress of Solitude. There was a sign on the front.

"Be right back – saving Gotham City."

Batman frowned. "He thinks *he's* saving Gotham City? Wait until he sees me take out the Joker with the Phantom Zone Projector."

Batman touched the communication device on his ear. "Kid? Did you get the projector?"

"Almost," Dick said. "There's these laser things blocking it, though."

"On it," Batman said. He knew how Superman powered his fortress. He made his way to the Knowledge Crystal Room and started breaking crystals at random. "First try!" he said to himself as he broke the fifth crystal. Then he coached Dick through a deadly obstacle course. Minutes later, the boy emerged with the Phantom Zone Projector.

"Got it, Bat-dad!" Dick said proudly.

"I told you, I am not adopting you," Batman said.

"Thank you very much, boys!"

Harley Quinn had grabbed the Phantom Zone Projector from Dick's hands. She pointed it at Batman.

"Mr J will be so happy when I tell him I sent you to the Phantom Zone, Batman!" she cheered. "Have a nice trip!"

There was a sound like thunder and a flash of

white light. Batman felt his body tingle as it began to dematerialize.

I probably should have listened to the kid! he thought.

THE END

CONTINUED FROM PAGE 150.

"I'm Batman," he replied. "I am not afraid of the dark. I *am* the dark."

He dropped down into the air duct. He slid down the chute ... and was stopped by a hunk of concrete at his feet.

Batman looked up. Harley closed the cover on the air duct. As he scrambled to get back up, he heard the sound of clinking chains. He pushed with all his might, but the cover didn't budge.

Then he heard Harley laugh.

"Sorry, Batman!" she said. "Guess you shouldn't have trusted me after all!"

THE END

CONTINUED FROM PAGE 31.

"Yeah, help them, sure," Batman said. "Come on! To the Batcopter!"

They piled into the Batcopter and quickly flew to Gotham City. Night was falling over Gotham City, and the lights from the tall buildings twinkled in the dark sky.

Batman came to a landing in the street in front of City Hall. A crowd of spectators had gathered there, and a news reporter was speaking into a microphone.

"The Joker is holed up in City Hall with the remaining villains who haven't been captured yet: Catwoman, Bane and Clayface," she said. "But members of the Justice League say they'll have City Hall cleared soon."

Batman pushed his way through the crowd, followed by Barbara and Dick. He saw Superman, Wonder Woman and The Flash standing in front of the City Hall steps.

"Batman! You're alive, old pal!" Superman said, slapping him on the back.

"Of course I am," Batman said. "Why wouldn't I be?"

"Well, we got word that the Joker and the Rogues had taken over Gotham City, and things were spinning out of control," Superman replied. "So of course we thought that you had been defeated."

"I haven't," Batman said. "So you guys can head out. I've got this."

"Who's your team?" Wonder Woman asked, nodding to Barbara and Dick behind him.

"They're not my team, they're my ... people who follow me around and help me fight evil," he answered.

"That sounds like a team to me," Wonder Woman remarked.

"Anyway, we'd better get moving," Superman said.

"The place is rigged with booby traps," Batman said. "Our best bet is to draw them out."

"How will we do that?" asked The Flash.

Batman didn't answer. He grabbed a megaphone from a police officer.

"Joker, come out here and face us!" he said.

The Joker's voice came through a speaker outside City Hall.

"And why should I do that, Batman?" he asked.

Batman remembered the Joker's words from the power plant. "Don't you want to face your greatest enemy?"

There was a pause. The door to City Hall burst open and the Joker stepped out, flanked by Catwoman, Bane and Clayface.

The Joker grinned. "Bring it on, Batman!"

The Super Heroes charged forwards.

Pow! Superman knocked Bane back with a powerful punch. The villain's strong muscles were no match for Superman's super-strength.

Crack! Catwoman sprang at Wonder Woman, cracking her whip. Wonder Woman jumped right over Catwoman! She spun around and lashed out with her magic lasso, wrapping it around Catwoman.

Whoosh! The Flash zoomed up to Clayface. There was a flurry of action as The Flash moved around the clay hero. He sculpted Clayface into the Statue of Liberty!

"That's a good look for you, don't cha think?" Flash asked, and Clayface growled.

At the same time, Batman raced up the steps towards the Joker.

Bam! The Joker raised his right fist, which was covered with a boxing glove. The boxing glove extended on a metal arm and hit Batman in the face! Batman stumbled backwards.

The Joker walked down the steps, grinning. He touched a purple flower on his green jacket.

"One squirt of my laughing gas and you'll be putty in my hands, Batman!" the Joker said. "This was too easy!"

Quickly, Dick did a flip, somersaulting through the air and snatching the flower off the Joker's jacket.

"Hey, get back here, kid!" the Joker yelled.

Batman jumped to his feet.

Pow! He pummelled the Joker, knocking him backwards. Barbara ran up and cuffed the Joker's hands behind his back.

"Game over," Batman said. "This city is back in the hands of the good people of Gotham."

The crowd cheered. Batman, Barbara and Dick climbed into the Batmobile and sped back to the Batcave. Inside, Alfred was watching a news report.

"Gotham City was just saved by a team of heroes led by Batman," the reporter was saying.

"Did you hear that?" Batman said. "*Led* by Batman. That's me."

"Your two new teammates seem to have been very helpful," Alfred said.

"You mean *our* new teammates," Batman said. He turned to Barbara and Dick. "What do you say? Will you two join our Bat team?"

"You bet we will!" said Barbara and Dick. They high-fived Batman and Alfred.

"What do we do now, Batman?" Dick asked.

"We order pizza," Batman replied. "Fighting evil makes me hungry!"

THE END

CONTINUED FROM PAGE 87.

Batman zoomed towards the waterworks in his Batwing and got there before Wonder Woman. Down below, he could see thugs emptying tanks of a green concoction from a lorry.

Then one of them looked up.

"Look up there! Batman's coming! Hurry!"

The thugs quickly started dumping the concoction into a big water tank. Batman landed the plane and jumped out as Wonder Woman landed behind him.

The Penguin walked towards him. "You're too late, Batman!" he cried. "The Joker may be captured, but his Operation Makeover is underway!"

"What's that?" Wonder Woman asked.

"When anyone in Gotham City takes a shower, their hair will turn green! Hwa, hwa, hwa!" the Penguin laughed.

Wonder Woman looked at Batman. "We could have stopped this if we had taken my jet!"

THE END

CONTINUED FROM PAGE 8.

Batman looked down at the energy core. Of course he had to choose the city. That's what he always did. Then he heard the Joker's voice.

"Guess I'll be flying away then, Batman," the Joker said. "Face it. You can try all you want, but you'll never catch me. Never!"

Never. The word echoed in Batman's brain. He didn't like that word.

Tick ... tick ... tick...

I'm Batman, he thought. *Why can't I do both? Just because the Joker says I can't?*

He swung up into the balloon.

"Never say never, Joker," Batman said, grabbing him by his purple collar.

The Joker's face turned even paler than usual.

Tick ... tick ... tick...

"Batman, you can't do this," the Joker said. "The energy core!"

"The energy core what?" Batman asked.

Boom! The Joker Bomb went off. The energy core exploded. The blast sent Batman flying out of the balloon...

"That was intense. It's a good thing I'm so strong, or that might have hurt bad," Batman said, sitting up.

Alfred – Bruce Wayne's butler, and the only one who knew his secret – gently pushed Batman back down.

"Take it easy, Master Bruce," Alfred said. "That was a huge explosion."

Explosion. It all came back to Batman. "The city, is it…"

"There was no major damage," Alfred replied. "The Joker Bomb didn't fully detonate, probably because it was installed by penguins. But the power is out. Luckily, Wayne Manor has a generator. I will start it."

"Good! I need to use the microwave," Batman said, sitting up again. He noticed that he was still in his Batsuit, with only the cowl removed from his head. Alfred must have helped him back to the Batcave after the explosion, he realized.

Suddenly, the lights in the Batcave flickered on. A TV screen came to life, revealing the Joker's grinning face.

"Citizens of Gotham City, the power is back on, and do you know who to thank? Why me, of course! Your new mayor! Mayor Joker!" he announced.

The camera pulled back to reveal the Joker sitting behind the desk in the mayor's office. Some of the Rogue villains surrounded him.

"Allow me to introduce you to my new staff," the Joker said. "First, my Deputy Mayor Harley Quinn."

"Deputy Quinn, at your service, Mr J!" Harley said, giving a big salute.

"My new police commissioner – Bane!" the Joker announced.

The big man grunted.

"And in charge of the Gotham City Water Utility – the Penguin," the Joker said.

The Penguin twirled his umbrella.

"Poison Ivy will run the Botanical Gardens. Scarecrow is now in charge of Arkham Asylum. Catwoman is our new Animal Control officer. And Killer Croc will run the Gotham City Aquarium."

Batman jumped up. "It's a bad day in

Gotham City when the villains run the show, Alfred!" he cried. "I've got to put a stop to this right now!"

Batman slipped the cowl back over his head and jumped into the Batmobile.

"Be careful, Master Bruce!" Alfred called out as the vehicle sped away.

Vrooom! Minutes later, Batman screeched to a stop in front of Gotham City Hall. The Joker's goons were lined up at the top of the front steps, guarding the front door.

Batman weighed his options. *I can smash my way through those guards,* he thought. Easy enough. *But maybe I need an element of surprise ...* His eyes drifted to the side of the building, where he saw a steel hatch door leading to the basement that was padlocked, but unguarded. Not as cool as rappelling up to the roof, but it was a way in.

Batman made his way to the door and used his batarangs to break off the lock. He opened the hatch and jumped in...

And found himself inside a box! He'd fallen right into a trap! Green and purple lights flashed

around him. On one wall were two levers: one purple and one green.

Batman knew the Joker's twisted mind well. One lever probably led to a way out. The other led to something really bad.

IF BATMAN PULLS THE GREEN LEVER, GO TO PAGE 137.

IF BATMAN PULLS THE PURPLE LEVER, GO TO PAGE 60.

CONTINUED FROM PAGE 26.

"Dick, that's genius!" Barbara exclaimed. "The initials spell out Aparo Park!"

"I was just gonna say that," Batman said.

They jumped into the Batmobile and headed to Aparo Park, a waterside park on the northern shore of Gotham. Batman pulled up.

"If I see one more drone, I'm going to blast it to pieces," he warned.

Dick pointed. "Look, Batman! Over there!"

The boy was pointing to a big sign with a question mark on it. It had been posted by some tall, green bushes.

"A hedge maze," Barbara said as they walked over to it. "I don't remember seeing this before."

"I think it's just for us," Batman said, and he stepped inside.

Barbara and Dick followed him. Inside the maze, the tall green hedges formed the walls of a twisting, turning labyrinth. Batman sped through it, making turns as he went.

Then he stopped. The hedge came to a three-pronged fork. One path led left. One path led straight. And the other path led right.

IF THEY GO STRAIGHT, GO TO PAGE 57.

IF THEY GO LEFT, GO TO PAGE 78.

IF THEY GO RIGHT, GO TO PAGE 161.

CONTINUED FROM PAGE 119.

Batman swam through the tube marked GROTTO. He emerged in a shallow pool, one of the aquarium habitats. He stuck his head out of the water ... and found himself surrounded by crocodiles! Real ones!

"Get him!" he heard Killer Croc growl. The crocodiles shot through the water like missiles.

Batman looked down at his Utility Belt, where he spotted a can of shark repellent.

"Rats!" Batman exclaimed. "Why don't I have croc repellent?"

There was nothing to do but fight. The crocodiles thrashed and splashed as Batman fought them off. Then he felt a hand on his shoulder.

"My turn, Batman!"

Killer Croc used one of his muscled arms to lift up Batman. He tossed him out of the grotto, onto the concrete floor outside the habitat.

Exhausted by fighting off the crocodiles, Batman still managed to jump to his feet. Killer Croc flattened him with a powerful kick and pressed his foot on Batman's chest.

"My next punch is gonna knock you out, Batman," Killer Croc warned. "And then I just might feed you to my crocs. They look hungry."

Batman struggled to break free. "You'll ... never..."

Bam! A blast of powerful water slammed into Killer Croc, knocking him backwards! Batman jumped up. Had Cyborg helped him?

No, it was the boy from the arena, holding the emergency fire hose.

"Hi, Batman," he said. "I'm Dick Grayson. I was here on a trip with the orphanage when this guy took over. And then..."

"One second, kid," Batman said.

Bam! He dazed Killer Croc and started to tie him up, just as Cyborg appeared.

"There you are, Batman," he said. "You got Croc? Awesome. I got all of the hostages out of here. Let's go take down another villain!"

"Yeah, well, I think I found another sidekick," Batman said. He nodded towards the kid.

Dick's eyes lit up. "Who, me?"

"You see anyone else here?" Batman asked.

"No! Wow, this is amazing!" Dick said. "Me, Dick Grayson, Batman's sidekick! The kids at the orphanage won't believe this. But I guess

I can't tell them. I need a secret identity, right? Do I get to wear a costume? I look really good in red..."

What did I just get myself into? Batman wondered.

THE END

CONTINUED FROM PAGE 123.

Batman and Barbara hopped in the Batmobile, and Batman drove to Brentwood Academy, a fancy private boys' school on the outskirts of Gotham City. Batman pulled up in front of the school and stepped out.

The Riddler's drone flew up to him and dropped another note.

Gotcha, Batman!

"Gotcha?" Batman asked.

Suddenly, a swarm of boys emerged from the school, surrounding Batman and Barbara. They all had spray-painted question marks on their school uniforms.

"You're captured, Batman!" one of the boys cried.

"Boys, why are you doing this?" Barbara asked.

"No more rules!" another boy answered. "We all live in Rogue City now. Come on, inside!"

Batman moved for his Utility Belt, but Barbara stopped him.

"You can't fight kids," she told him.

"I can't?" Batman asked.

"We'll have to play along for now and figure out some way out of here later," she answered.

THE END

CONTINUED FROM PAGE 150.

"I'm not afraid of the dark," Batman said. "I *am* the dark."

He moved to go down the chute, then stopped.

"Wait a second," he said. "That's just the kind of thing someone would say to try to get me to go first. I'm not doing it. You first, Harley. That's it."

"If you insist, Batman!" she said cheerfully. Then she stopped. "Ya know, I'm thinking maybe I don't like this chute so much. Let's try *that* chute."

She pointed to another air duct.

"See ya down there!" she said, and then she climbed in and disappeared.

Batman followed her down the chute. He slid down the metal tube like a kid on a water slide. The chute dropped him into a small, confined space. He landed on his feet. In the darkness, he could make out Harley in front of him. She held a finger to her lips.

They were in a wardrobe, Batman realized. Through the wardrobe door, Batman could hear voices.

"Now where was I on my list of new laws?" the Joker was saying.

"Number thirty-five, boss," one of his thugs replied.

"Ah yes. Thirty-five," said the Joker. "No loud noises before ten a.m. No children laughing! No dogs barking! I need my beauty sleep. Now, for number thirty-six…"

Harley Quinn leaned towards Batman. "What are you waiting for?" she asked. "Do your Batman stuff!"

"Right," Batman said. Thanks to Harley, he had the element of surprise – a great advantage.

Bam! He kicked open the closet door.

The Joker's head spun around.

"Batman!" he cried. "Get him!"

One of the Joker's goons lunged towards Batman, wielding a club. Batman grabbed the club out of his hand.

Wham! He flipped over the goon like a pancake, sending him skidding across the floor.

A second goon charged at Batman, holding a mallet.

Pow! Batman sent him flying backwards with a hard kick.

A third goon jumped on Batman's back. Batman hurtled himself backwards.

Whack! He slammed the goon against the wall. The unconscious goon slid down to the floor.

He turned to face the Joker, who had his hand on a fake, green flower on his jacket.

"Take one step, Batman, and you'll be sleeping like a big baby," the Joker threatened.

Batman quickly slipped a gas mask over his nose and mouth.

"I came prepared, Joker," he said.

The Joker frowned. He produced a gun in his other hand.

"Were you prepared for this, Batman?" he asked.

Schwing! A batarang zipped through the air and knocked the weapon from the Joker's hand.

"Always," Batman said. Then he lunged. In just a few quick movements, he had the Joker's hands behind his back and locked in bat-shaped handcuffs.

"Noooo!" the Joker wailed.

That's when Harley Quinn stepped out of the wardrobe.

"Hiya, Mr J!" she said cheerfully.

"Harley!" the Joker wailed. "You were supposed to help me capture Batman!"

"I tried, but I guess it didn't work," she said with a shrug. "And now I have another idea. You sounded like you were having a lot of fun being mayor. I think I'd like to be mayor, too. Mayor Harley Quinn. It's got a ring to it, don't it?"

"And how do you think you're gonna make that happen?" Batman asked.

Harley grinned. "Like this!"

She produced an enormous mallet out of nowhere, and swung it at him.

IF BATMAN JUMPS TO THE LEFT, GO TO PAGE 113.

IF BATMAN JUMPS TO THE RIGHT, GO TO PAGE 160.

CONTINUED FROM PAGE 47.

Batman raced straight ahead without talking to Barbara or Dick. The path emerged into a clearing – and standing there was a man wearing a mask over his eyes, a green bowler hat and a green suit decorated with question marks.

"The Riddler!" Batman cried.

"Batman! You found me," the Riddler said.

"What's this about, Riddler?" Batman asked.

The Riddler shrugged. "Now that the bad guys are in charge, I'm bored," he said. "I thought it would be fun to send you on a wild goose chase."

"Yeah. A real riot," Batman said flatly.

Then the Riddler pointed his question mark-shaped cane at Batman. "Capturing you is just a bonus!"

"You'll have to try harder than that, Riddler," Batman said. His BatRope whipped out and wrapped around the cane, yanking it from the Riddler's hands. Then he launched himself at the Riddler.

Bam!

One martial arts kick brought the Riddler

down. Batman was tying the Riddler's hands behind his back when Barbara ran up.

"Sorry, Batman," she said. "I turned my head and Dick wasn't there. I think he's lost in the maze."

"He seems like a clever kid," Batman said. "I'm sure he'll find his way home."

Barbara shook her head. "You are hopeless!" she said, and took off to find the missing boy.

The Riddler grinned. "Looks like it's just you and me, Batman!"

THE END

CONTINUED FROM
PAGE 141.

Batman jumped left and landed in soft grass. He saw a sign on the wall of the habitat.

Lin-Lin

Giant Panda

Batman turned to see an enormous, cuddly, white-and-black panda next to him. The panda knocked Batman down! Then it put its head down on Batman and started snoring.

Perched on the nearby wall, Catwoman laughed. "He's using you as a pillow, Batman. How *purrr*-fectly sweet!"

Batman struggled to get the heavy panda off him. "You won't get away!" he yelled to Catwoman.

"No, *you* won't get away," she replied. "At least, not until Lin-Lin is done with her nap!"

Then she disappeared over the edge of the wall.

THE END

CONTINUED FROM PAGE 44.

Batman pulled the purple lever. The floor opened beneath his feet! An unseen force pulled him through a tube at rocket speed. The tube deposited him in a clear capsule, and then shot out into … water?

The river, Batman realized. *The tube must have taken him through the sewer system.*

The capsule was rapidly sinking. Batman reached for his Utility Belt. All he had to do was cut through the glass capsule, and he could swim to the surface.

Before he could start, he saw a blur in the water next to him. Then he felt the capsule being lifted up and out of the water.

The capsule broke through the surface, and Batman saw a figure in red and blue holding the capsule.

"Superman!" Batman exclaimed, but it wasn't a happy exclamation.

Superman flew to the shore and deposited the capsule on a dock by the river. Batman saw other heroes from the Justice League standing there: Wonder Woman and Cyborg.

Superman used his heat vision to quickly burn a hole through the capsule. Batman stepped out.

"I could have saved myself, you know," Batman said.

"You're welcome!" Superman said cheerfully.

"So, what are you guys doing in Gotham City, anyway?" Batman asked.

"Well, we were all … hanging out, and we heard that Gotham City was in trouble," Superman replied.

"Hanging out? Like a party or something?" Batman asked.

Wonder Woman and Cyborg looked away.

"No, of course not, Batman," Superman said. "Anyway, here we are! We can help you take back Gotham City from the Joker."

"I don't need any help," Batman said. "Gotham City is my city. I can do it myself."

"Sure," Wonder Woman said. "That's why you ended up in the river."

Batman grunted. "So I guess you're going to help me, whether I want you to or not?" he asked.

"Exactly, old friend!" Superman said. "Our plan is to take down the Rogue villains, and then go after the Joker. We were going to split up, but why don't you team up with me?"

"Or me!" Cyborg said.

Wonder Woman shrugged. "You can team up with me, if you want, I guess," she said.

IF BATMAN TEAMS UP WITH SUPERMAN, GO TO PAGE 89.

IF BATMAN TEAMS UP WITH WONDER WOMAN, GO TO PAGE 130.

IF BATMAN TEAMS UP WITH CYBORG, GO TO PAGE 117.

IF BATMAN GOES BACK TO THE BATCAVE AND TEAMS UP WITH ALFRED, GO TO PAGE 139.

CONTINUED FROM PAGE 138.

"B.G. and H.Q.," Batman mused. "It's completely impossible to figure out who might have sent those notes."

"Master Bruce, I suspect that H.Q. might be Harley Quinn," Alfred suggested. "The initials give it away. And also the jester hat sticker on the envelope."

"Like I said, completely impossible," Batman said. "I'll pick one at random … B.G."

"Very good, Master Bruce," Alfred said.

The note from B.G. asked to meet in the park next to the Gotham City Library. Batman sped there, parked the Batmobile, and waited.

"Batman."

He looked out the window to see a serious-looking woman with dark red hair.

"You're Commissioner Gordon's daughter, Barbara Gordon," Batman said. "Sorry, I can't talk right now. I'm waiting for someone called B.G."

"*I'm* B.G.," Barbara replied. "Let me in. We need to talk."

Batman unlocked the passenger door. "Make it quick, Barbara. I've got a city to save."

"That's what I wanted to talk to you about,"

Barbara said. "The Joker and his Rogues – they've captured my father. I want your help to get him back – and take back the city from these villains."

"Don't worry, I'm on it," Batman said. He revved the engine of the Batmobile. Barbara didn't move.

"You can go now," Batman said.

"I'm not going anywhere!" Barbara insisted. "After my father's retirement tomorrow, I'm slated to take over as police commissioner."

"You?" Batman asked.

"I was police chief in Blüdhaven for years," Barbara said. "I cleaned up the streets there. I can do the same for Gotham City. But these Rogues are too much for our police force. I need your help."

"I've told you, I got this," Batman replied.

"You're not doing this without me," Barbara told him. "They've got my father. This is personal."

A memory flickered in Batman's brain. His own mother and father had been taken out by a street thug when he was just a boy. It was why he became the Batman. Every time he fought a villain, it was personal.

"Fine," Batman said. "You can tag along. But I am a one-man team. You are just ... someone who is not on the team but rides along."

"Whatever you want to call it," Barbara said. "Now let's go to City Hall and bust out my dad!"

"The whole place is booby-trapped," Batman told her. "We need another plan."

Barbara looked thoughtful. "Maybe if we take down the Rogues, one by one, the Joker will fall."

"That will never work," Batman said. "What we should do is take down the Rogues, one by one, so the Joker will fall."

"That's what I just said," Barbara protested. "And I think I know where we should go first. We should – hey!"

The passenger door swung open and Batman pushed her out. "You are not acting like a non-team member. Sorry. Batman flies alone."

Then he zoomed away through the streets of Gotham City. He was going to take down the Rogues, and thanks to the Joker, he knew just where to find them all.

IF BATMAN GOES AFTER POISON IVY FIRST, GO TO PAGE 135.

IF BATMAN GOES AFTER SCARECROW FIRST, GO TO PAGE 172.

CONTINUED FROM PAGE 13.

Batman was torn. He knew Superman could probably take care of himself. But the Joker had tied him up with ropes infused with Kryptonite. The hero might be in real trouble.

Muttering under his breath, Batman bolted out of the mayor's office and pounded on the goons carrying Superman away.

Pow! Bam! Wham! He knocked them out one-two-three. Then he unwound the ropes from around Superman's body.

Superman let out a breath. "Thanks, Batman."

"Let's go," Batman said. "We can take the Batwing."

"Good idea," Superman said. "I'm still weak."

Batman pressed a button, and he and Superman raced outside. Moments later, the sleek black Batwing landed next to Batman. He and Superman climbed inside.

"See? I can fly, too," Batman said, as the small jet took off. Then he pressed a button on the dashboard. "And, it's got great sound."

Music pulsed through the cockpit as they sped towards Superman's Fortress of Solitude. They arrived just in time to see the Joker emerging from a helicopter with Harley Quinn and the Penguin.

Batman landed the Batwing, and he and Superman charged towards the villains.

The Penguin spotted them first. "Ah, it's that meddlesome man in the mask!" he cried. "And his flying friend!"

The Penguin aimed his umbrella at them, shooting them across the icy landscape. The projectiles bounced right off Superman's chest.

"Curses!" the Penguin cried as Superman scooped him up. He tossed the Penguin across the ice, and he landed in a heap.

"That's not very nice!" Harley Quinn yelled. She ran towards Superman holding a large mallet. Batman leapt through the air and grabbed onto the handle of the mallet. Then he flipped Harley Quinn like a pancake.

The Joker, meanwhile, was running towards the Fortress of Solitude. Superman flew towards him, but Batman hurled a batarang at the Joker. The batarang reached the Joker first, and he went down in a heap.

Superman scooped him up.

"What should we do with these guys?" Superman asked.

"Let's bring them to Arkham Asylum," Batman suggested. "We'll have to take it back from Scarecrow, but that shouldn't be a problem."

When they arrived at Arkham, they saw police cars out front, their red lights spinning. Commissioner Gordon was standing outside, along with his daughter, Barbara.

Batman jumped out of the Batcopter and ran to the commissioner.

"Is everything all right?" he asked.

"It's excellent, Batman," Gordon replied. "Barbara rescued me from the Joker. Then we came here and brought down the Scarecrow, rescuing Gotham City's police officers."

"I took down the Joker," Batman reported.

"I helped!" Superman added.

"Thanks, Batman," Barbara said. She stepped up to shake his hand. "I'll be taking over as police commissioner soon, now that my dad is retiring. I have a lot of ideas for how we can work together. Can we talk?"

"Some other time," Batman said. "I've got some important things to do."

"Bye, Batman!" Superman called out as Batman took off in the Batwing.

Batman flew back to the Batcave, where he watched some TV and ate some leftover Lobster Thermidor. The next morning, Alfred brought him the newspaper.

"You made the front page, Master Bruce," Alfred told him.

Batman read the headline: *Superman and Batman Save Gotham City!*

He scowled. "Couldn't they have at least put our names in alphabetical order?"

THE END

CONTINUED FROM PAGE 26.

Batman, Barbara and Dick headed for t
amusement park. When they got there, the wor
"CLOSED" was spray-painted over the sign. But the
front gate was open.

They stepped inside the eerie, empty park.

"Look!" Dick cried, pointing.

The teacup ride – giant teacups on a spinning
platform – was covered in spray-painted, purple
question marks.

"The Riddler!" Batman said, jumping up on the
platform. Barbara and Dick followed him.

Then they heard the groaning of gears, and the
platform began to spin!

"Quick! Into the cup!" Barbara yelled, and they
all dove into a giant teacup and held on.

"How do we stop this thing?" Dick asked.

"Don't worry. I'll get us off this crazy ride," Batman
promised as the ride spun around and around.

If I don't lose my lunch first! he thought.

THE END

CONTINUED FROM PAGE 133.

Batman jumped into the mine cart on the right-hand track. Wonder Woman jumped into the seat next to him.

"That's not how splitting up works," Batman said.

"I know," Wonder Woman said. "But the Joker has probably set up an elaborate trap for us on one of these paths. It's better if we stick together."

"Fine," Batman replied. He pulled the lever on the cart, and it rolled along the track into the dark mine.

The mine cart twisted and turned through the mine. They came to the end of the track – and found Commissioner Gordon trapped inside a glass box!

"Commissioner!" Batman cried. He and Wonder Woman jumped out of the mine cart and rushed towards him.

"Batman! Wonder Woman!" Commissioner Gordon cried. His voice was muffled through the glass, and his eyes looked worried behind his glasses. "Be careful! This box is booby-trapped!"

He nodded towards two levers on the outside of the box, numbered ONE and TWO.

"One of them will open the door," Gordon said. "And the other will open the floor."

Batman looked down. The glass box was hanging off the edge of the track. Down below, a pit of strange, green mud bubbled, looking really gross.

"Don't worry," Batman said. "I'll pick the right lever."

IF BATMAN CHOOSES LEVER ONE, GO TO PAGE 110.

IF BATMAN CHOOSES LEVER TWO, GO TO PAGE 86.

CONTINUED FROM PAGE 174.

Batman pressed a button on his wrist device and waited. A few minutes later, the sleek black Batcopter landed next to him and Barbara, as silently as a bird in flight.

"Stealthy," Batman said. He hopped into the cockpit and Barbara sat next to him.

The Batcopter lifted up and quietly sailed over the fence. Most of the buildings of Arkham were topped by tall, peaked spires, but one of the side buildings had a flat roof. The Batcopter landed.

Whoosh! Clouds of Scarecrow's green fear gas exploded from the roof.

"It's motion activated!" Batman cried, and then he and Barbara began to cough.

"Fly away!" Barbara yelled, but Batman was suddenly overcome by fear – the fake fear produced by the Scarecrow's gas.

"I can't!" Batman said. "We'll crash!"

He jumped out of the cockpit. Barbara did, too. Then she screamed and pointed.

"Look!"

A cute, brown sparrow hopped along the edge of the roof.

"It's going to peck us!" Barbara cried. "Hide!"

She raced around the helicopter and she and Batman ducked behind the copter.

"It's horrible," Batman whispered. "Those beady little eyes ... that sharp little beak..."

"What should we do?" Barbara asked. "We've got to get out of here!"

"We're not going anywhere!" Batman replied. "Not while that creepy bird is out there!"

THE END

CONTINUED FROM PAGE 47.

"Let's go left!" Dick said. "I've got a good feeling about this."

Batman, Barbara and Dick took the left path. It twisted and turned several times and then emerged into a clearing. Standing there was a man wearing a mask over his eyes, a green bowler hat and a green suit emblazoned with question marks. He carried a yellow question mark–shaped cane in one hand.

"The Riddler!" Batman cried.

"Batman, you made it!" said the Riddler. "And you brought some friends with you."

"They're not my friends," Batman said. "We just hang out."

"But it's not fair," the Riddler said. "I was hoping for a Riddler versus Batman blowout, and now it's three against one."

"If one-on-one is what you want, that's what you'll get," Batman said, and he lashed out with his lasso. It wrapped around the Riddler's cane and jerked it from his hands. Then…

Bam! Batman flattened the Riddler with a martial arts kick.

"How'd that work out for you, Riddler?" Batman said as he tied the villain's hands behind his back. "I've got a nice cell in Arkham waiting for you."

The Riddler giggled. "That's only if you can get out of my maze of mystery!" he said.

Dick held up a little snack bag filled with jelly beans. "That's no problem. I started a jelly bean trail on the way in."

"Curses!" the Riddler cried.

They made their way out of the maze and delivered the Riddler to Arkham Asylum. When they returned to the Batmobile, Batman looked at his dashboard and frowned.

"I've got to go to the Batcave to refuel," he said. "Can I drop you guys off somewhere?"

"Nope!" Barbara and Dick answered.

Grumbling, Batman took off for the Batcave. Dick pressed a button on the dashboard.

"Hands off, kid," Batman warned as the voice of a radio announcer filled the vehicle.

"This just in! The Justice League is in town, and they're taking back Gotham City!" the announcer said. "They're taking down the Rogue villains one by one."

"No, *I'm* doing that," Batman protested.

"That's good news," Barbara said. "We could use some help."

"*I* don't need any help," Batman snapped.

They quickly reached the Batcave. Dick jumped out and gazed around in wonder.

"Wow, the Batcave! Awesome!" he said, running around.

"If you guys are gonna hang with me, you've got to look the part," Batman said. He walked over to a big wardrobe. "I've got some old stuff in there for you, kid. Barbara, there's a box of extra Bat swag. Find something."

"Cool!" Dick cried.

Batman got busy refueling the Batmobile. Another radio report blared.

"Looks like the Justice League is heading to Gotham City Hall," the announcer said. "They've got their sights set on the Joker."

"This calls for the Batcopter," Batman said. "You guys ready?"

"Ready!" Barbara and Dick cried.

Dick had on a red uniform top, short green shorts, a yellow cape and black goggles over his eyes. Barbara wore a cowl with bat ears and a yellow cape over her purple-and-yellow uniform.

"You two don't look as cool as me," Batman said. "But we have no time. We've got to stop the Justice League."

"Don't you mean *help* the Justice League?" Barbara asked.

IF BATMAN TRIES TO STOP THE JUSTICE LEAGUE SO HE CAN SAVE GOTHAM CITY HIMSELF, GO TO PAGE 96.

IF BATMAN HELPS THE JUSTICE LEAGUE, GO TO PAGE 32.

CONTINUED FROM PAGE 136.

Batman plucked the blue flower and held it under Barbara's nose. She breathed in the fragrance.

Immediately, her skin began to turn blue.

Poison Ivy laughed. "Wrong flower, Batman!"

Batman plucked the red flower and tried that, but it didn't work. The blue color was creeping all over Barbara's skin. He picked her up and carried her to the Batmobile.

"Later, Batman!" Poison Ivy called out. "Next time come alone so we can spend some quality time together."

Batman gritted his teeth and sped off towards the Batcave. He hated to let another Rogue villain get away – but he had no choice. He had to save Barbara.

THE END

CONTINUED FROM PAGE 138.

"I think I'll meet this H.Q.," Batman said. "H.Q. stands for headquarters, right? Maybe this person knows how to get into City Hall."

"Master Bruce, it's more likely that H.Q. stands for—" Alfred began, but Batman was already speeding out of the Batcave.

Batman sped through Gotham City and turned down a dark alley, following the GPS coordinates on the note. He stopped at a dead end and waited.

He heard a faint noise – was that bells? And suddenly, an upside-down face appeared in front of him, peering through the windshield.

"Batman! You came!"

"Harley Quinn!" Batman said. "So you're H.Q."

Harley Quinn jumped down from the roof of the Batmobile. She wore a red-and-black jester costume with pigtails and roller skates.

"Who else would I be, Batman?" she asked, leaning in through the window.

Batman put the Batmobile in reverse. "Forget it, Harley. Whatever you're selling, I'm not interested."

"What if I'm selling revenge – revenge on the Joker?" she asked.

Batman stopped. "Keep talking."

"My Mr J is like a chicken sitting on a nest right now, Batman," Harley said. "He thinks nobody can take him down. But *we* can."

Batman's eyes narrowed. "We? Why would you want revenge on the Joker?"

Harley pulled out a long scroll and unravelled it. In scrawled hand, on the top, were the words, "Why I Want Revenge on the Joker".

"You want me to read them all?" Harley asked.

"Not necessary," Batman said. "You're about as trustworthy as a cat babysitting rats, Harley. I'm sure this is one of your old tricks."

"And what if it is?" Harley asked. "Are you telling me that big, strong Batman with all of his awesome gadgets can be tricked by little old Harley Quinn?"

"Well," Batman said slowly. She was making a lot of sense.

"Let's work together, Batman," Harley said. "I know all of Mr J's secrets. We can capture him. If I try to trick you, you'll just stop me, right? So it's a win-win."

"So you can get me inside City Hall?" Batman asked.

"I got an even better idea," Harley said. "Let's blast the Joker into the Phantom Zone! Then he'll never bother us again!"

IF BATMAN CONSIDERS HARLEY QUINN'S PROPOSAL TO SEND THE JOKER INTO THE PHANTOM ZONE, GO TO PAGE 101.

IF BATMAN AND HARLEY QUINN RETURN TO CITY HALL, GO TO PAGE 148.

CONTINUED FROM PAGE 75.

Batman pulled lever two. The door swung open. "Told you," Batman said.

"Thank you, Batman!" Commissioner Gordon said. "I can't believe the Joker's plan to take over Gotham City has succeeded. Have you stopped him yet?"

Wonder Woman spoke up. "The Justice League arrived in Gotham City to help, sir. We've got our best people on it. We should check in with them."

"If the Joker is still out there, he's mine," Batman said.

But when they met up with the Justice League, Superman had news for them.

"Gotham City is saved!" he announced. "I've captured the Joker. And the rest of the Justice League has cleared Gotham City of all villains!"

"Of course you did," Batman grumbled.

Then Commissioner Gordon's walkie-talkie crackled.

"Commissioner! There's a strange lorry

loaded with tanks heading right for the water-works!"

"Nothing to worry about," said Superman. "We took down the Penguin, and…"

"Um, I didn't take down the Penguin," Cyborg said. He looked at Wonder Woman. "Did you?"

"Not me," Wonder Woman said.

"Uh-oh," said Superman.

"I'm on it," Batman said.

"I'm with you," said Wonder Woman.

Batman jumped in his Batwing. Wonder Woman jumped into her Invisible Jet.

"Seriously, Batman, my jet is better for this mission," Wonder Woman said.

IF BATMAN STAYS IN HIS BATWING, GO TO PAGE 38.

IF BATMAN JUMPS INTO THE INVISIBLE JET, GO TO PAGE 91.

CONTINUED FROM PAGE 147.

Batman dodged Clayface. He jumped onto a bucket-loader machine and slid behind the controls. He pulled a lever, raising the heavy steel loading bucket. Then he drove forwards.

"Aaaargh!" Clayface angrily charged the bucket loader.

Bam! Batman brought the bucket down on Clayface, pinning the clay villain to the ground. Then he jumped out of the driver's seat.

"Sorry to flatten you and run, Clayface," Batman said, "but I've got a city to save."

"Nice job, Batman," Barbara complimented him, as they returned to the Batmobile.

"Of course," Batman said. "Now let's head north and find the Riddler."

GO TO PAGE 24.

CONTINUED FROM PAGE 62.

Batman thought about it. If Superman took out all the villains by himself, he'd get all the credit.

"I'll stick with you, Superman," Batman said.

"Fantastic, old buddy!" Superman said. "You know what I'm thinking? Let's not wait. Let's take down that Joker!"

"Sounds good to me," Batman said. He pressed a button and his Batmobile pulled up.

"I can fly there," Superman reminded him.

"If we're doing this together, then let's do this together," Batman said. *So you don't get there before me and take down the Joker by yourself,* he thought.

Superman hopped into the Batmobile. "Let's do this, Batman! See ya later, guys!"

He waved to Wonder Woman and Cyborg as they sped away.

"So I have to warn you," Batman said. "Joker's got the whole place booby-trapped."

"No problem!" Superman said. "I can find the booby traps with my X-ray vision."

"Yeah, well ... I may not have X-ray vision, but I have awesome night vision goggles," Batman said.

"Good for you," Superman said. "Of course, I can always *fly* over City Hall to look for traps."

"I can fly, too – with my Batwing," Batman countered.

"And then I can use my super-strength to take down any of the Joker's guards," Superman said, flexing his right bicep.

"Do your muscles have cool tools?" Batman asked, motioning to his Utility Belt.

They had reached City Hall.

"Batman, we still don't have a plan," Superman said. "I say I fly us both up to one of the windows and get in that way."

"I say we forget about sneaking and just bust in there," Batman argued.

IF SUPERMAN FLIES UP TO A WINDOW WITH BATMAN, GO TO PAGE 11.

IF SUPERMAN AND BATMAN JUST BUST IN THERE, GO TO PAGE 129.

CONTINUED FROM PAGE 87.

Batman hopped into Wonder Woman's Invisible Jet. She zoomed away, and soon they were flying above the waterworks. Down below, Batman could see a lorry pulling up to a water tank. In the back of the lorry were tanks full of a green concoction. The Penguin waddled up to the lorry.

What's going on down there? Batman wondered.

Wonder Woman flicked an invisible switch, and the voices from below filled the cockpit.

"The Joker may be captured, but he'll have the last laugh," the Penguin said. "Once we dump this stuff into the water tank, anyone who takes a shower in Gotham City will end up with green hair!"

"Ugh!" said Wonder Woman. "That's a crime against coolness. Let's stop this."

She parked the silent Invisible Jet behind a nearby water tank. The Penguin and his thugs had no idea they'd been spotted. They talked and joked as they unloaded the lorry.

Bam! Batman appeared out of nowhere and started taking down thugs.

Whoosh! Wonder Woman wrapped her lasso around the Penguin.

"Sorry to crash this diabolical party," Batman said. "But the fun is over."

They delivered the Penguin to Arkham Asylum and then returned to City Hall, where the Justice League was helping Commissioner Gordon get resettled.

"Batman! Did you get the Penguin?" Superman asked.

"We did," Batman said. "So you guys can go now."

"But we should celebrate," Cyborg piped up. "We could—"

"Seriously," Batman said. "Thanks and everything, but you know – just … go."

The Justice League members took off, and Batman gave a sigh.

Gotham City was his once more.

THE END

CONTINUED FROM PAGE 147.

Pow! Batman swung at Clayface. His arm became absorbed by the villain's gooey clay body.

"Gee, Batman, I didn't know you were stuck on me," Clayface taunted, in his deep, gravelly voice.

Batman tried to pull out his arm, but it was stuck. Even worse, his whole body was getting pulled into Clayface's massive form, as though he were sinking in quicksand.

"Batman!" Barbara cried. She grabbed his free arm and pulled, but it was no use.

Clayface laughed. "You can't escape me!"

"This … is … so … not cool!" Batman cried as he struggled to get free.

Now Barbara was slowly getting sucked into the clay, too. "Let us go!"

"No way!" said Clayface. "You two are sticking with me until the Joker decides what to do to you!"

THE END

CONTINUED FROM PAGE 171.

"Surrender? Never," Batman said. "I am going to put an end to the Joker's games once and for all."

"Then let me help you," Catwoman said.

"Sorry, but I'm not in the mood to trust super-villains today," Batman said. "You're going to Arkham."

Catwoman sighed. "I know there's a soft heart under all that armour somewhere," she said.

"Don't be so sure," Batman replied.

Batman, Catwoman and Alfred squeezed into the Batmobile and sped off towards Arkham Asylum. They found the place swarming with Gotham City police officers. Barbara Gordon, Commissioner Gordon's daughter, was standing outside.

"Hello, Batman," she said. "We've secured the facility."

"What about Scarecrow?" Batman asked.

"He's contained," Barbara replied. "We were about to go rescue Superman."

"That's my job," Batman said.

"Are you sure you don't need any help?" Barbara asked.

"He's sure," Catwoman answered for him.

Officers took Catwoman away, and Batman and Alfred zoomed towards City Hall.

"What's your plan, Master Bruce?" Alfred asked.

"This," Batman replied.

He stepped on the gas and steered the Batmobile up the steps of City Hall and through the doors! He jumped out of the Batmobile – and heard laughter behind him.

"Nighty night, Batman!" said the Joker.

Batman smelled something strange – and then everything went black. When he opened his eyes, he saw he was in a sealed room with Alfred, Superman, Wonder Woman and Cyborg.

"I think perhaps you need another plan, Master Bruce," Alfred said.

THE END

CONTINUED FROM PAGE 81.

"Yeah, help them, sure," Batman said. "Come on! To the Batcopter!"

They piled into the Batcopter and quickly flew to Gotham City. Night was falling over Gotham, and the lights from the tall buildings twinkled in the night sky.

Batman hovered above City Hall. A crowd of spectators had gathered there, and a news reporter was speaking into a microphone. He could see Superman, Wonder Woman and The Flash standing in front of the crowd.

Batman's eyes narrowed. "Saving Gotham City is *my* job," he said.

He ejected from the helicopter and released a black parachute. Then he floated down to City Hall.

"Step aside, Justice League," he said. "Batman is here to..."

Bam! A soccer ball with a Joker face came barrelling through the air, aimed by one of the Joker's thugs on the roof. He went spiralling through the air and managed to grab the leg of the Batcopter to control his flight. Dick helped him into the copter.

"Good thing I'm a good pilot," Barbara said. "That was a close one."

"Just a minor setback," Batman said. "I can still..."

"Look!" Dick cried.

Down below, Superman was flying out of City Hall, carrying the Joker. Barbara hit a switch on the dashboard of the copter, and sound filled the cockpit.

"The Justice League has saved Gotham City!" a reporter has announced.

"Sorry, Batman," Barbara said. "You didn't get to save the day this time."

"But look on the bright side," Dick added. "You've got us."

Batman smiled at them. "You're right!"

THE END

CONTINUED FROM PAGE 168.

A metal arm extended from the Bat-Sub. It turned the big gear. One tube opened up. Water started pouring into the cube!

"Looks like it's time for plan B," Batman said.

Batman ejected from the sub and swam over to the cube. He put a small explosive on the cube. Then he motioned for Alfred to stand back.

Alfred obeyed. The carefully controlled explosion went off, blasting a hole through the cube. Batman reached in and grabbed Alfred. Then they swam to the water's surface.

As he and Alfred emerged, sputtering for air, Batman saw the Penguin standing over them, on a floating dock in the middle of the reservoir.

"Gotcha, Batman!" the Penguin cried.

A net fell on both of them, entangling them, and the penguin minions swam to them, surrounding them.

"Thank you, Master Bruce," Alfred said.

"No problem. And we'll get out of this, too," Batman said, but he was thinking something else:

I sure hope these penguins are nicer than they look...

THE END

98

CONTINUED FROM PAGE 8.

Batman thought about it. He knew he would have another chance to get the Joker. But he only had one chance to save the city.

"If you'll excuse me," Batman told the Joker, "I've got to defuse that bomb."

Batman let go of the Joker and dropped back down to the energy core. He quickly defused the bomb before time ran out. When he emerged from the power plant, the crowd outside clapped and cheered.

Commissioner Gordon ran up to him.

"Batman, you saved Gotham City once again!" he said. "We should celebrate! Today's my last day on the job, you know."

"Sorry, I can't," Batman said. "I've got a date."

That's not technically a lie, Batman thought. *I do have a date – a date with some leftover food and my couch. But Gordon doesn't have to know that.*

Then he jumped into the Batmobile and sped away, satisfied with saving the city one more time.

THE END

CONTINUED FROM PAGE 85.

"Messing with the Phantom Zone is a dangerous idea," Batman said.

"Sure it is," Harley Quinn said. "But you gotta take a risk if you want to do something great, don't cha? If you put Mr J in the Phantom Zone, he'll never be able to escape. You'll be done with him forever!"

The idea was tempting – too tempting. Batman opened the passenger door.

"Get in," he said.

"Whee! I get to ride in the Batmobile!" Harley cheered as she climbed in.

Batman backed out of the alley.

"So how do you propose to open up the Phantom Zone?" he asked.

"You know how, silly," Harley replied. "Superman's got a Phantom Zone Projector in his Fortress of Solitude. You just aim it at Mr J and zap! He's gone forever."

"Computer, I need plans for the Fortress of Solitude," Batman said, and a holographic image appeared between him and Harley. "Looks like

Superman's got the Phantom Zone Projector stashed so nobody can get to it."

Harley pointed to the holographic blueprints. "There's a pipe, see? It's narrow, but if you can find someone to crawl through it, bingo! The projector's yours."

At that moment, Batman was driving past the Gotham City Orphanage. A small boy was swinging from the bottom of a tree branch.

"Someone small, eh?" Batman asked. He stopped the Batmobile and got out.

"Hey, kid, do you want to help me save Gotham City?" he asked.

The boy's eyes grew wide. "Me? Dick Grayson? Help you, Batman?"

"That's the idea," Batman said.

"Of course I will!" Dick said. "But we need permission first. Come on!"

Dick grabbed Batman by the hand and dragged him into the orphanage. After meeting with the principal, they came back outside.

"This is amazing!" Dick said. "It's almost like you're adopting me, Batman! I won't let you down. I've got a lot of useful skills."

"I am not adopting you," Batman insisted.

"Well, you're adopting me for this mission, right?" Dick asked.

"Just for this mission," Batman said. "Right."

"So what kind of mission is it?" Dick asked, as they walked to the Batmobile.

"We're going to borrow the Phantom Zone Projector from Superman's Fortress of Solitude," Batman replied.

"Borrow?" Dick asked. "But isn't that—" He stopped when he saw Harley Quinn. "What's *she* doing here? Isn't she a villain?"

"Yeah, but borrowing the Phantom Zone Projector was a good idea," Batman said.

Dick looked at Batman. "Gosh, Batman, I don't know about this. Messing with the Phantom Zone Projector sounds awfully dangerous. And are you sure you can trust Harley Quinn?"

IF BATMAN TELLS DICK NOT TO WORRY, GO TO PAGE 28.

IF BATMAN AGREES THAT DICK HAS A GOOD POINT, GO TO PAGE 124.

CONTINUED FROM PAGE 152.

"All right. What did your book say to do?" Batman asked.

"I think we're supposed to tickle the vines," Barbara said. "Like this." She moved her fingers, tickling the closest vine. It shrank away from her. "It's working!" Barbara cried, tickling another vine.

"No way. Batman does not tickle," Batman said.

"It's the *only* way!" Barbara said.

Barbara was almost free. Batman grudgingly reached for one of the vines with his fingers and tickled it. It shrank away from him, too.

Fully free now, Barbara tickled the vines around Batman until they were both free. Then she immediately tackled Poison Ivy.

"You can't tickle your way out of these!" Barbara said, slapping handcuffs on her wrists.

At that moment, a Gotham City police car sped up and two officers came out.

"Ms Gordon!" one of them said. "We got your call. Bane has commandeered most of the police vehicles, but a few of us got away. And Scarecrow has taken over Arkham Asylum."

Barbara nodded towards Poison Ivy. "Keep her in your police car for now. Batman and I will take care of Bane."

"I can handle Bane by myself," Batman said. "I don't need—"

A screen flashed on the communication device on Batman's wrist. A face appeared – the face of the Penguin.

"Hello, Batman," the Penguin said.

"What do you want, Penguin?" Batman asked.

"Money, and lots of it," the Penguin replied.

The screen flickered and a new image appeared. It was Alfred! He was tied up in a chair...

The Penguin's face appeared again.

"Tell Bruce Wayne that I've got his butler," the Penguin said. "He can have him back – for a hundred million dollars. And I want *you* to bring me the money."

Then the screen went blank.

Batman's mind was racing. The Penguin didn't know Batman's true identity. He couldn't know how much Alfred meant to him. *He's setting a trap for me,* Batman thought, *and getting some money out of Bruce Wayne at the same time.*

Batman raced to the Batmobile and jumped in. Barbara Gordon got into the passenger seat. He looked at her.

"I'm going to save Alfred," he said. "Alone."

"You *need* me, Batman," Barbara argued. "I got us out of those vines back there, didn't I? I'm not going anywhere. And if you ditch me here, I'll just follow you again."

Batman was worried about Alfred – and in too much of a hurry to argue.

"Fine," he said. "But if you're gonna hang with me, you've gotta look the part."

He picked up a long tube. "I don't go anywhere without my merch gun."

Whomp! Whomp! Whomp! Batman shot the merch gun into the air. Official Bat gear flowed down. A cowl. A cape. A uniform with a bat on it.

Barbara quickly suited up, and then Batman raced to the Gotham waterworks, where he hoped to find the Penguin. He drove to the facility, and he and Barbara jumped out of the Batmobile.

"Freeze, Batman!"

A bold man wearing a refrigerated suit of armour faced them.

"Mr. Freeze!" Batman cried, racing towards him.

"I said, freeze!" Mr. Freeze repeated. Then he aimed a freeze blaster at them.

Boom!

IF BATMAN AND BARBARA DODGE TO THE RIGHT, GO TO PAGE 128.

IF BATMAN AND BARBARA DODGE TO THE LEFT, GO TO PAGE 165.

CONTINUED FROM PAGE 75.

Batman pulled lever one.

Whoosh! The floor dropped out from under Commissioner Gordon's feet. He started to plummet.

Batman quickly pulled lever two and dove after Gordon. His cape billowed behind him as he zoomed after his target. He reached out and grabbed Gordon in a bear hug.

Wonder Woman's magic lasso whipped out and wrapped around Batman and the police commissioner, stopping their fall inches above the bubbling green mud. Then Batman shot his grappling hook to the top of the precipice and pulled them both up to safety.

"Thank you, Batman," Commissioner Gordon said. "Thanks, Wonder Woman. You saved me."

"No problem," Batman said. Then he started lowering himself back down the precipice.

"Batman, what are you doing?" Wonder Woman asked.

"Saw something down there," Batman said, without further explanation.

He swung down and saw a tunnel in the wall just below and jumped into it. Ahead, something glowing and green had caught his attention when he was diving after Commissioner Gordon.

As he approached, he heard voices.

"Operation Makeover is underway," someone said. "Once we dump this stuff into the water supply, everyone in Gotham City will have green hair!"

Batman got closer and saw some of the Joker's thugs loading tanks of green liquid onto the back of a lorry. He leaped forward.

"I've got a new name for your operation," he growled. "Operation Bad Day. Because you're all about to have one!"

The thugs lunged at Batman.

Bam! Pow! Whack! He sent each one flying with punches and kicks. But one got away and the lorry took off with a screech.

Batman ran after it. The lorry zoomed out of the tunnel, onto an open road outside the mines. It was getting away!

Then the lorry came to a stop. But why? Batman couldn't see anything on the road.

Then Wonder Woman and Gordon stepped out of the Invisible Jet.

"Need help, Batman?" Wonder Woman asked.

The thug driving the lorry kicked open the door and started to run.

"No, thanks. I got this," Batman said. He hurled a batarang at him and knocked him down.

Commissioner Gordon was reading the labels on the barrels in the back of the lorry.

"Good thing you stopped this, Batman and Wonder Woman," he said. "You two would make a great team!"

The two Super Heroes looked at each other – and grinned.

THE END

CONTINUED FROM PAGE 55.

Batman jumped to the left, avoiding the mallet. Harley swung again. Batman reached out and grabbed the handle in mid-swing.

Bam! The giant hammer hit the floor, but Batman didn't let go of his grip. He wrestled it out of Harley's hands.

"Hey, that's mine!" Harley wailed.

Batman quickly pulled her hands behind her back and cuffed her.

"Thanks for leading me right to the Joker," he said. "I knew all along that you were trying to trap me. But I don't trap easily."

Harley shrugged. "You can't blame a girl for tryin'!" she said cheerfully. "What're you gonna do now, Batman?"

"I'm gonna give Gotham City back to the people," he promised.

He methodically travelled around the city, taking down the Rogues one by one.

Bam! He flattened Bane and returned the police department to Commissioner Gordon.

Pow! He ejected the Penguin from the waterworks.

Slam! Wham! Whack! He rounded up Killer Croc, Captain Boomerang, Catwoman, Poison Ivy, Clayface and the Riddler – all by himself.

When he had rounded up every last Rogue, he brought them to Arkham Asylum. He found Barbara Gordon, the daughter of Commissioner Gordon, out front. Her eyes grew wide at the sight of the captured Rogues with Batman.

"Batman, you've been busy!" she said. "I took Arkham back from the Scarecrow. It's all ready for you."

"Thanks," Batman said. "But I could have taken down the Scarecrow myself."

"Uh, you're welcome?" Barbara said.

Gotham City's finest helped Batman lock each and every Rogue in a cell in the creepy asylum. Batman jumped into his Batmobile and sped back to the Batcave.

Once there, he slipped off his cowl and popped some leftover Lobster Thermidor into the microwave.

"Computer," he said out loud. "Calculate the chance of the Joker escaping this time."

After a few seconds pause, the computer replied, "100 per cent."

The microwave dinged. Batman took out the leftovers and settled into an armchair. Of course the Joker would escape. That's the way things worked.

He turned on the TV and *Real Arguing Ladies of Gotham City* came on the screen. He took a bite of lobster and examined his thoughts.

Life was good. He'd saved Gotham City. Locked away the villains, for now. And he was chilling with good TV and awesome leftovers. So why didn't he feel happy?

There's something missing, he realized. *Maybe one day I'll figure out what it is.*

THE END

CONTINUED FROM PAGE 62.

Batman reconsidered Cyborg. He might be young, but the kid did have a pretty cool laser eye. And he wouldn't try to boss Batman around or anything.

"I'll take Cyborg," Batman said.

"All right! The Borg and the Bat," Cyborg said.

"Yeah, whatever," Batman said. His Batmobile zoomed up to the dock, and Batman motioned for the Cyborg to climb in.

"You two head to the aquarium," Superman said. "We got word that Killer Croc is causing some trouble there."

"This is my city. I'm calling the missions," Batman said. He turned to Cyborg. "We're going to the aquarium. Killer Croc is causing some trouble there."

"You got it, Batman!" said Cyborg.

They sped to the Gotham City Aquarium and got out of the Batmobile. They walked inside the large building. Enormous glass tanks held all kinds of fish, sharks and sea creatures on display for the public to view.

But the place was eerily quiet.

"There's nobody here," Cyborg said.

Then a speaker crackled to life.

"Welcome, visitors, to the Rogue City Aquarium," a sinister voice greeted them. "Be sure to enjoy our latest exhibit in the aquarium arena … the performing Gotham citizens!"

Batman and Cyborg raced to the arena, an outdoor area with bleachers surrounding a large pool. In the middle of the pool was a platform, and on the platform was a group of huddled, scared people. Sitting in a tall chair above them was Killer Croc, the green, scaly, crocodile-like villain.

"Killer Croc, let those people go!" Batman yelled.

Killer Croc laughed. "Batman! My first customer," he said. "You're just in time for the first show."

"This is pretty cruel, Croc," Cyborg said.

"Cruel?" Croc asked. "Isn't it cruel to keep animals in tanks, just so citizens can gawk at them? Well, now the tables have turned!"

A boy bravely stepped out from the group of terrified tourists.

"Mr Croc, sir, I'm happy to perform," he said. He did a triple backflip. "See?"

Some of the tourists applauded weakly.

"You're not supposed to be happy," Killer Croc growled. "Let's see you do that trick in the water!"

He jumped off the chair, about to push the boy, but Batman was faster. He sent his grappling hook to a pipe overhead, and then swung to the platform, knocking over Killer Croc before he could push the boy. Then Batman and Killer Croc tumbled into the water.

Croc was a fast swimmer, faster than Batman. He rocketed through the water and seemed to disappear into the wall.

When Batman got closer, he saw large holes in the wall, each one leading into a large pipe. Killer Croc must have swum through one of them. But which one?

IF BATMAN SWIMS INTO THE PIPE MARKED GROTTO, GO TO PAGE 48.

IF BATMAN SWIMS INTO THE PIPE MARKED TANK, GO TO PAGE 162.

CONTINUED FROM PAGE 158.

Batman pulled the wire from the blue port. The Mind Control Machine sparked and sizzled.

Batman and Barbara pulled off their metal beanies.

"We did it!" Barbara cried, and Batman raced out of the office into the hallway.

The halls were crowded with the citizens of Gotham City that the Rogues had captured and stashed in Arkham – police officers, members of the former mayor's staff and other good guys. They all looked around, confused.

"Where are we?" someone asked.

The lights flickered and Scarecrow appeared at the top of a staircase.

"You're locked away in Arkham Asylum!" he cackled. "And that's where you're going to stay!"

Batman stepped through the crowd. "We've fried your Mind Control Machine, Scarecrow!" he announced. "Surrender now!"

Scarecrow just grinned. He held up a remote-control device. "I've got other tricks up my sleeve, Batman. All I have to do is press this button, and the entire building will be flooded with Fear Gas!"

His finger moved towards the button. Then something whizzed through the air, knocking the remote from his hands. But it wasn't one of Batman's batarangs. He spun around and saw Barbara behind him.

"A stapler from the office," she said. "I improvised."

"Knocking stuff out of people's hands is my deal," Batman growled.

Barbara pointed behind him. "Batman, he's going for the remote!"

Batman spun around. He whipped out his BatRope and lashed out at Scarecrow. The lasso wrapped around his legs, tripping him. Batman ran over to Scarecrow and pinned him down.

A group of police officers ran up to help.

"We'll take it from here, Batman," one of them said.

"Good idea," Barbara told them. "We'll round up the rest of the Rogues and bring them here. Make sure Scarecrow gets a secure cell."

"Noooooo!" Scarecrow wailed.

"What's the matter, Scarecrow?" Batman asked. "Scared?"

He got up and turned Scarecrow over to the officers. Then he strode outside.

"Batman, wait up!" Barbara cried. She ran to catch up with him. "So, who should we go after next?"

Before Batman could answer, a drone came

flying towards them. It stopped in front of Batman and hovered there. Batman noticed that the drone had question marks all over it.

The bottom of the drone slid open and a note dropped into Batman's hands. He opened it and read it out loud:

> *Riddle me this, Batman!*
> *I'll Grant you the honour of finding me,*
> *If you can guess just where I'll be.*
> *You'll find boys here during the day.*
> *But after dark, they cannot stay.*

"A place where boys go during the day," Batman said. "Hmm. He could be talking about a boys' school. Brentwood Academy!"

Barbara looked over his shoulder. "Maybe, but why is the word 'Grant' capitalized? I bet it means Grant Park!"

IF THEY LOOK FOR THE RIDDLER IN BRENTWOOD ACADEMY, GO TO PAGE 51.

IF THEY LOOK FOR THE RIDDLER IN GRANT PARK, GO TO PAGE 15.

CONTINUED FROM PAGE 103.

Hearing the words from the kid's mouth made sense. Trusting Harley Quinn, stealing the Phantom Zone Projector – none of those sounded like good ideas.

"That was the old plan," Batman said. "I was about to tell you my awesome new plan. And that is how I'm going to use Harley Quinn to get close to the Joker."

"Sure, whatever you want, Batman," Harley Quinn said.

"Now here's the plan…" Batman began.

A short while later, Harley Quinn marched up the steps of City Hall with young Dick Grayson.

"Tell Mayor J I got a surprise for him," Harley said.

One of the goons guarding the door disappeared and returned a moment later. He let Harley Quinn and Dick inside, and they marched to the mayor's office. The Joker sat in the mayor's chair with his feet on the desk.

"Harley! Where have you been? I sent you out to

bring me Batman," he said. "This is no bat. This is more like … a little bird."

"This is better than Batman," Harley said. "This is Batman's kid. We got ourselves a hostage!"

"Batman's kid?" the Joker asked.

"Dick Grayson, sir, former orphan," Dick told him.

The Joker laughed. "This is brilliant! A hostage! We'll have Batman eating out of the palm of my hand."

"Glad you like it, Mayor J," Harley said.

The Joker looked at Dick. "And why would Batman adopt a kid like you?" he asked.

"I've got skills," Dick said.

Saying that, he somersaulted through the air, over the Joker's head, landing behind him. Then Dick threw open the window.

Whoosh! Batman flew in, his black cape billowing behind him. He knocked the Joker out cold before the villain could say a word.

"Great plan, Batman!" Dick said.

"Yeah," Harley Quinn said, "except for one thing. You shouldn't have trusted me!"

She produced an enormous mallet and brought it down on Dick. The boy nimbly dodged out of the way.

Batman grabbed the mallet from her. Dick tripped her and she fell to the floor.

"Good work, kid," Batman complimented him.

"Thanks, Bat-dad," Dick said.

"I told you I'm not—" Batman started to say but then he stopped.

A few hours later, after the Joker, Harley Quinn and the rest of the Rogues were safely inside Arkham Asylum, Batman and Alfred watched Dick Grayson run around the Batcave.

"This is amazing!" Dick said. "I get to be Batman's sidekick. I was thinking I need a Super Hero name. How does Robin sound?"

"Like the bird?" Batman asked.

"Yeah, like the bird," Dick said. "I'll need a costume, too." He ran to Batman's closet. "Wow! Look at these."

Alfred looked at Batman and smiled. "Well done, Master Bruce. Well done."

THE END

CONTINUED FROM PAGE 108.

Batman and Barbara dodged to the right to avoid the icy blast.

Barbara somersaulted, and the blast missed her. But it hit Batman. He became immediately frozen in a giant block of ice!

Batman couldn't move. He couldn't speak. He could see Mr. Freeze's evil grin through the ice, and from the corner of his eye, he saw Barbara running away.

Maybe she'll come back and unfreeze me, he thought. *She does kind of seem to be good at crime-fighting stuff.*

THE END

CONTINUED FROM PAGE 90.

Batman charged up the City Hall stairs.

Bam! Pow! He knocked out the two goons guarding the door. Then he kicked in the front door and ran inside. Superman followed him.

Whomp! A cage dropped down from the ceiling, trapping both of the heroes. Superman grabbed the bars – and then quickly let go.

"Kryptonite!" he cried.

"Guess you can't count on your super-strength, can you?" Batman taunted.

"Maybe not, but do you have anything in your Utility Belt that can cut through Kryptonite?" Superman asked.

Batman paused. "Um, maybe."

"That's what I thought," Superman said. "I hope we can find some way out of this. I don't want to end up as the Joker's permanent pets!"

THE END

CONTINUED FROM PAGE 62.

Batman weighed his options. Superman could be well … annoying. Cyborg was okay, but he was young…

"I'll go with you, Wonder Woman," he said. "I'll just call for my Batwing."

"We don't need it," Wonder Woman replied. "We can take my Invisible Jet."

Batman paused. "My Batwing is much cooler."

"I don't think so," Wonder Woman replied.

"But it has cool gadgets," Batman protested.

"So does mine," Wonder Woman countered.

"Yeah, but you can't see them," Batman argued.

Wonder Woman glared at him. "I'm going to police headquarters to take down Bane. If you want to help me, meet me there."

She walked off towards her Invisible Jet.

Batman called for his Batwing, and moments later the sleek black craft arrived and landed next to him. He waved goodbye to Superman and Cyborg and took off for police headquarters.

When he arrived, he saw Wonder Woman waiting for him. Two goons in jeans and muscle shirts were standing in front of the doors, their arms folded.

The two heroes walked up to the goons.

"Stop right there, you two," one of the goons said, blocking their path.

"We can do this the easy way or the hard way," Batman told them.

"No, you're gonna do it Bane's way, Batman," the goon said. "He's gonna—"

Pow! Batman flattened the goon with a karate move.

Bam! Wonder Woman took out the other goon.

"They always choose the hard way," Batman said.

The two heroes stormed into police headquarters. There were no police officers in sight – just Bane's goons, goofing off.

Batman came to a door with a plaque that read, "Commissioner Jim Gordon." He kicked it open.

A huge, muscled man jumped up to face them. He wore black wrestling tights with thin shoulder straps. Angry red eyes gleamed from behind a black wrestling mask that covered his face. His arms and legs were as thick as tree trunks.

"Bane! What have you done with Commissioner Gordon?" Batman asked.

"Why should I tell you?" Bane growled. He kicked the desk between him and Batman and it exploded into splinters.

Batman knew he couldn't compete with Bane's super-strength. He needed a gadget or a gimmick to subdue the big villain. Something like…

"Tell the truth, Bane!" Wonder Woman cried. She swung her magic lasso at Bane, wrapping him in it. Even his big muscles couldn't resist the power of the lasso.

"Where is Commissioner Gordon?" Wonder Woman asked.

Several more goons stormed into the room.

Pow! Bam! Batman took care of them while Wonder Woman pressed Bane.

"Where is he?" she asked again.

Bane tried to resist, but he couldn't. "The … abandoned … mines," he said slowly, through gritted teeth.

The last goon dropped to the ground. Wonder Woman looked at Batman.

"What do we do with him? Is there a prison cell here that will hold him?" she asked.

"Not for long," Batman said. "But a nice nap will slow him down."

He took a small can from his Utility Belt and sprayed it in Bane's face. The big man went out like a light.

Batman and Wonder Woman locked up Bane, and Wonder Woman removed her magic lasso. Then the two of them hurried to the abandoned mines just outside Gotham City. Two tunnels led into the underground mines.

"We've got to find Commissioner Gordon," Batman said. "We should split up."

IF BATMAN AND WONDER WOMAN SPLIT UP, GO TO PAGE 154.

IF BATMAN AND WONDER WOMAN STICK TOGETHER, GO TO PAGE 74.

CONTINUED FROM PAGE 67.

Batman drove to the Gotham Botanical Gardens. Thick green vines were entwined around the metal front gates.

A woman with green eyes and bright red hair walked up to him as he exited the Batmobile.

"Batman! Have you come to admire my lovely plants?" Poison Ivy asked.

"Plants are boring," Batman replied. "I've come for you, Poison Ivy. This garden belongs to the good people of Gotham City."

"Nature belongs to everyone!" Poison Ivy said. She stretched her arms out wide. "Plants, help me eject this intruder!"

Two giant yellow flowers turned towards Batman. They opened up to reveal jaws full of big teeth, like lions. The flowers lunged at Batman. He dodged out of the way.

"Batman!" Barbara Gordon raced up. She grabbed Poison Ivy and then flipped her, sending her flying. Then she hit one of the lion flowers with a martial arts kick.

"Leave my plants alone!" Poison Ivy ran up to

Barbara, furious. She held up a plant mister and sprayed the contents in Barbara's face. *Achoo!* Barbara's eyes fluttered and she started sneezing over and over again.

Batman ran to Barbara.

"Antidote," she gasped, pointing to two flowers along the path. One was blue and the other was red.

IF BATMAN USES THE RED FLOWER TO HELP BARBARA, GO TO PAGE 151.

IF BATMAN USES THE BLUE FLOWER TO HELP BARBARA, GO TO PAGE 82.

CONTINUED FROM PAGE 44.

Batman pulled the green lever.

Whomp! The walls of the box collapsed around him. When the dust cleared, Batman saw a tall man in a blue flight uniform standing in front of him.

"G'day, mate," the man said in an Australian accent.

"Captain Boomerang, right?" Batman asked. "What's your deal? You throw boomerangs?"

"That's right, mate," Captain Boomerang replied.

Batman removed a bat-shaped object from his Utility Belt. "Big deal," he said. "I've got a batarang."

"It looks like a boomerang," Captain Boomerang said.

"No, it doesn't," Batman shot back. "It's shaped like a bat. That makes it better."

He hurled the batarang at Captain Boomerang. The Australian villain ducked and twirled around, quickly shooting several boomerangs at Batman.

Boom! Boom! Boom! The boomerangs started to explode all around Batman.

"Mine are better," Captain Boomerang said. "Mine explode!"

Batman's batarang returned to his hand. He quickly jumped out of the basement. He slammed the steel hatch doors shut.

Boom! Boom! Boom! They safely exploded behind the doors.

Batman jumped back into his Batmobile. City Hall was probably loaded with booby traps, he guessed. He sped home. He needed a new plan.

Alfred was waiting for him when he returned to the Batcave. As he jumped out of the car, Alfred pulled something off the windshield.

"There are two notes here, Master Bruce," Alfred said. "One is signed B.G. The other is signed H.Q. They are both asking you to meet with them. How mysterious."

IF BATMAN MEETS WITH B.G., GO TO PAGE 65.

IF BATMAN MEETS WITH H.Q., GO TO PAGE 83.

CONTINUED FROM PAGE 62.

"No, thanks," Batman said. "I'll do this on my own."

"That's fine, Batman," Superman said. "Can you take care of Catwoman? We've got the rest covered. Let's all meet at City Hall when we're done."

Before Batman could agree or disagree, Superman flew up into the air. Wonder Woman flew off in her Invisible Jet, taking Cyborg with her.

Batman was all alone on the pier – without a vehicle. Before he could call the Batmobile to him, it zoomed up. The door swung open and Alfred stepped out!

"Master Bruce, I was worried about you," he said. "Your tracking device showed you at the bottom of the river. I assumed the worst."

"I'm fine, Alfred," Batman said, not mentioning that Superman had saved him. "I'm going to take down Catwoman at the Gotham City Zoo."

He climbed into the Batmobile driver's seat. Alfred slid into the seat next to him, and Batman looked at him.

"Well, I certainly can't take a taxi back to Wayne Manor," Alfred said. "The city has been taken over by villains."

"Fine," Batman said, as they sped off. "Just don't get in my way."

When they got to the Gotham City Zoo, the gates were wide open. People were running out, yelling.

"Oh dear!" exclaimed Alfred. "It looks like some trouble is brewing."

"You can say that again," Batman said. He stopped the Batmobile and stepped out. Alfred followed him, and they stepped through the gates of the zoo.

Once inside, it was easy to see the source of the chaos. Lions, cheetahs and leopards were freely roaming the zoo grounds! Catwoman was patting the mane of a large lion.

"Nice kitty," she purred.

"Catwoman! Are you serious? This is super dangerous," Batman said.

"Nice to see you, Batman," she said. Her green glowing eyes peered at him through her goggles. "Isn't this nice! These poor little kitties are free now."

"Free to cause mayhem," Batman said. "They belong behind bars. And so do you."

Catwoman jumped up. "Just try and catch me, Batman!" she cried.

She jumped up on a tall stone wall bordering one of the animal habitats. With amazing agility, she ran along the narrow edge, away from Batman.

Batman jumped up on the wall after her. "Alfred, round up these big cats!" he called down.

"But Master Bruce, I—"

Batman ignored him and chased after Catwoman. She made a turn, running down a wall between two of the habitats. Batman caught up to her and lashed out with a martial arts kick.

She jumped up, avoiding it, and landed steadily on her feet. Then she flipped right over Batman's head!

He spun around, losing his balance. Catwoman lunged at him.

IF BATMAN JUMPS LEFT TO AVOID HER, GO TO PAGE 59.

IF BATMAN JUMPS RIGHT TO AVOID HER, GO TO PAGE 169.

CONTINUED FROM PAGE 13.

Batman made a quick decision. Yes, Superman was in trouble. But he could take care of himself, right?

He raced downstairs, summoning his Batwing as he ran. Moments later it landed outside City Hall. Batman hopped in and zoomed towards Superman's Fortress of Solitude.

The icy palace, located on the frozen tundra, glimmered beneath the starry sky as Batman approached. He saw that a helicopter had already landed. The Joker, Harley Quinn and the Penguin emerged from it.

Batman landed his Batwing.

"Stop right there!" he called out to the three villains.

The Joker laughed. "Look! That pesky bat has flown all the way to Superman's hideout. Do you really think you can stop us, Batman?"

"Yes," Batman replied, and he charged towards the villains.

The Penguin aimed his umbrella weapon at Batman, releasing a hail of projectiles. Batman wrapped his cape around him, and the projectiles bounced off.

"Nice try, Penguin," Batman said. Then…

Bam!

Everything went black.

When he opened his eyes, he saw Harley Quinn standing over him, holding her giant mallet.

"That's gonna hurt in the morning, Batman," she said, grinning.

He sat up, groggy. He wasn't sure how long he'd been out, but he saw the Penguin's robotic minions waddling across the ice, towards the Joker's helicopter. They were holding up a gleaming metal device with a lens on one end that looked like a red eye.

"The Phantom Zone Projector!" Batman cried.

He jumped up. The Penguin had grabbed the projector from his minions. They waddled onto the helicopter, and the Penguin and Harley Quinn jumped in. The Joker was already at the controls.

"See ya, Batman!" he called out over the roar of the helicopter's engine. "Too bad you won't have a Gotham City to go back to!"

"Nooooo!" Batman grabbed onto the helicopter's landing skids as it lifted up.

He hung on with all his might as the copter

made its way back to Gotham City at super-speed. He couldn't pull himself into the cockpit.

When they reached Gotham City, he heard the Joker's voice.

"Put it in reverse, Deputy Quinn!" he called out.

"You got it, Mayor J!" Harley replied.

Light shot from the Phantom Zone, illuminating the night sky. A huge, swirling vortex opened up overhead. Batman watched as the vortex began to suck up all of Gotham City's power lines. The whole city went dark.

"Oops. Oh man, that's not good," Batman said to himself.

THE END

CONTINUED FROM PAGE 16.

Batman and Barbara headed twenty blocks south – and found themselves at a rock quarry on the edge of town. Huge construction vehicles were parked next to piles of rocks and rubble, but no workers could be seen. Giant boulders lined the quarry.

"Riddler? Are you here?" Batman called out.

One of the boulders suddenly started to move. It transformed into a huge, hulking clay body with thick arms and legs. Yellow eyes glowed from his clay face, and his mouth was a gaping maw.

"Clayface!" Batman cried.

The hulking villain charged towards him. "Nice to see you, Batman! The Joker will be happy once he hears I've captured you!"

IF BATMAN DODGES CLAYFACE, GO TO PAGE 88.

IF BATMAN FIGHTS CLAYFACE, GO TO PAGE 93.

CONTINUED FROM PAGE 85.

"Messing with the Phantom Zone is dangerous," Batman said. "Let's break into City Hall."

"Suit yourself!" Harley said, and then she flung open the door and hopped into the passenger seat.

Tyres screeched as the Batmobile zipped backwards out of the alley.

"Wheeeeeee!" Harley Quinn squealed gleefully.

They sped across town, but Batman slowed down as they neared City Hall.

"The Joker has the place booby-trapped," Batman said.

"I know that," Harley said. "But he ain't got nothing up on the roof. All we gotta do is climb."

Batman drove around to the back of City Hall. He and Harley Quinn got out of the Batmobile. A tall iron fence stood between them and City Hall. Batman climbed to the top and peered over. Four guards paced back and forth in the yard.

"We can get up to the roof," Batman said. "But I've got to take down the guards first."

"All we need is a distraction!" Harley said, climbing up next to him. "Watch!"

She tossed something over the fence.

Pop! Pop! Pop! Fireworks exploded above the guards' heads. They were completely distracted by the pretty lights.

Batman quickly launched his grappling hook onto the roof and securely attached the other end to the fence. Then he attached Harley Quinn to himself with a safety clip and began to pull them both up the roof.

"Whe—" Harley began, but Batman stopped her midsqueal.

"Shhhh!" Batman warned, nodding down to the guards.

They quickly reached the roof, and Batman unhooked Harley. She marched over to an air duct on the roof and removed the cover.

"This is how we get in," she informed him.

"You first," Batman said.

"No way!" Harley protested. "It's dark and creepy in there."

This could be a trap, Batman thought.

"I'll be right behind you," he said. "Ladies first."

"Ha!" Harley said. "So polite, Batman. Not like Mr J. But I can't go down first. It's too creepy!"

"You hang out with the Joker," Batman said. "You should be used to creepy."

"What's the matter, Batman?" Harley asked. "Are you afraid of the dark?"

IF BATMAN LETS HARLEY GO FIRST, GO TO PAGE 52.

IF BATMAN GOES FIRST, GO TO PAGE 31.

CONTINUED FROM PAGE 136.

Batman quickly plucked the red flower and held it under Barbara's nose. Her eyes fluttered, and she stopped sneezing.

"Thanks, Batman," she said.

Poison Ivy sneered. "How sweet. No flowers for me, Batman?"

"The only thing I have for you is a cell at Arkham Asylum," Batman answered, standing to face her. "And there aren't any flowers there."

"I see you're not a nature lover, Batman," Poison Ivy said. "Perhaps I can persuade you. Plants, give Batman and his friend a nice big hug!"

The thick green vines whipped away from the front gates and wrapped around Batman and Barbara Gordon. Batman felt his chest tighten as the vines squeezed him like a cobra.

"They're going to squeeze us to bits, Batman!" Barbara cried, struggling to get free of the vines.

"I've got it covered," he said. His hands were pinned to his body, but he could still reach his Utility Belt. "Once I reach my batarang, I'll slice our way out of this."

"Batman, I've done some research on Poison Ivy," Barbara told him. "I remember reading about these vines of hers. Slicing them is only going to cause us more problems."

"Who's the hero here?" Batman asked. His fingers reached his batarang. He could feel the sharp edge with his fingertips – perfect for slicing through the vines.

"Batman, no!" Barbara cried.

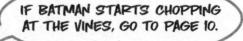

IF BATMAN STARTS CHOPPING AT THE VINES, GO TO PAGE 10.

IF BATMAN AND BARBARA FIND SOME OTHER WAY TO ESCAPE THE VINES, GO TO PAGE 105.

CONTINUED FROM PAGE 133.

"One of these paths could be a trap," Wonder Woman warned.

"I know," Batman replied. "But I'm not afraid of the Joker's traps."

He hopped into the mine cart on the left-hand side.

"First one to rescue Commissioner Gordon wins," he said, and then pulled the cart lever. It rolled into the dark caverns...

... and then, *whoosh!* The track stopped sharply, and he hurtled into the darkness. Then he felt the cart drop. The track had come to an end.

Thinking quickly, he threw his grappling hook into the darkness. Luck! It latched onto a craggy rock in the side of the mine. He grabbed onto the ropes tightly and let the mining cart drop.

It crashed loudly into the Earth far, far below him.

Batman turned on a flashlight and assessed the situation. He was dangling from his grappling hook above the cavernous mine. If he dropped, he'd be doomed. He tried swinging from side to side, but the rope wasn't long enough to get him to the walls of the mine.

His next thought made him frown.

I bet Wonder Woman could help me get out of this!

THE END

CONTINUED FROM PAGE 174.

"Where's this underground entrance?" Batman asked.

"Follow me," Barbara said.

Batman followed her a block away to an old phone box on a seedy street corner. Barbara went inside.

"Dad told me about this," she said. "It's a secret way in and out."

"It looks like a phone box," Batman said. "Who uses phone boxes any more?"

Barbara pressed some numbers on the pad of the payphone. The floor began to sink, as if they were in a lift. They slowly dropped down into a dark tunnel.

"This leads to the main office," Barbara whispered. "We might find the Scarecrow there."

They followed the tunnel to a set of stone steps. The steps ended at the door. Batman moved to kick it down but Barbara stopped him. She put a finger to her lips and put her ear to the door.

Batman took a small sound amplification device from his Utility Belt and put it to his ear. Then he listened, too.

"I'm so pleased to welcome all you new residents of Arkham Asylum!" the Scarecrow was saying over the PA system. "Police officers, members of the former mayor's staff. Don't waste your time thinking of a way to escape. Thanks to my Mind Control Machine, your only thoughts will be what I tell you to think!"

The Scarecrow cackled with glee. Batman peeked through the small glass window in the door. A strange contraption with crackling wires sat on the desk in front of the Scarecrow.

Batman ducked down. "He must be using that machine to alter the brain waves of everyone inside Arkham," he said. "We've got to shut it down!"

"If we go in there, the machine will zap our brains, too," Barbara pointed out.

Batman produced two round, metal beanies. He placed one over the cowl on top of his head. "These will protect us."

"Where do you keep all this stuff?" Barbara asked. But she put the metal beanie on her head, too.

Batman spied through the window until the Scarecrow left the office. Then he opened the door, motioning for Barbara to follow him.

Blue energy sparked from the machine when they approached.

"Doesn't this thing plug in?" he asked, looking around it.

"It must be powered by an independent energy core," she said. "Maybe we could short it out by pulling out the wires."

She pointed to the base of the machine. One wire was plugged into a red port on the back of the machine. The other one was plugged into a blue port. Barbara frowned.

"Hmm," she said. "I wonder if it makes a difference which one we take out first?"

IF THEY PULL OUT THE WIRE IN THE RED PORT FIRST, GO TO PAGE 17.

IF THEY PULL OUT THE WIRE IN THE BLUE PORT FIRST, GO TO PAGE 121.

CONTINUED FROM PAGE 55.

Batman jumped to the right.

Bam! Harley Quinn's mallet came down on his head. His world went black.

When he opened his eyes, he saw a bare lightbulb swinging overhead. The air smelled dank and musty. He was in a room with peeling paint on the walls. The door had one small, barred window near the top.

Batman jumped to his feet and moved to the door. He tried to open it, but it was locked. He looked through the window – and saw the laughing face of Scarecrow staring back at him.

"Welcome to Arkham Asylum, Batman!" the Scarecrow crackled.

THE END

CONTINUED FROM PAGE 47.

"This way!" Batman said, running down the path on the right. Barbara and Dick followed him.

They immediately turned right again. Then they turned left. Then right. Then left. They turned and turned until finally Batman stopped.

"I'm beginning to think this whole maze is a trap!" he said. "The Riddler is up to his old tricks."

"I'm sure we can figure it out, Batman," Dick said hopefully.

"We'd better," said Barbara. "Who knows what the Joker and the super-villains are doing to Gotham City while we're stuck here!"

THE END

CONTINUED FROM PAGE 119.

Batman swam into the tube marked TANK. He emerged into a huge aquarium tank – filled with sharks! They lazily swam back and forth around the tank. Batman could see rows of sharp teeth in their mouths. But so far, they hadn't noticed him.

Batman reached for his Utility Belt and grabbed a can of Shark Repellent. He shook it. It was empty!

The sharks all turned towards Batman at once. He shot up to the surface, but they surrounded him. Then they lunged...

A red laser beam hit the sharks one by one, pushing them away from Batman. He looked up to see Cyborg standing on a platform at the top of the tank. He had a sleeping Killer Croc by the back of the neck in one hand. In the other was a barrel-shaped laser blaster.

The top of the tank was high overhead, so Batman used his grappling hook to escape from the water. He landed on the platform, gasping.

"You okay, Batman?" Cyborg asked.

"I'm fine," Batman replied, jumping to his feet.

"Those sharks were about to eat you!" Cyborg said. "I guess I saved your life."

"Ummm, sure," Batman grumbled.

Cyborg nodded down to Killer Croc. "I took care of this guy, too. Guess we should hook up with the rest of the Justice League and see what's what."

"Whatever," Batman said.

They brought Killer Croc to Arkham Asylum. Superman was there, holding a captured Bane. Wonder Woman had captured Scarecrow. The Flash appeared, holding a captured Penguin.

"Great job so far, everyone!" Superman said. "We're almost done. We need to capture the Riddler and the Joker."

"The Joker is mine," Batman said. He marched back to his Batmobile. Cyborg shoved Killer Croc at Superman and followed Batman.

Batman zoomed to City Hall. "The place is booby-trapped," he told Cyborg.

Cyborg held up his blaster and grinned. "That shouldn't be a problem."

And it wasn't. Cyborg blasted through the gates of City Hall. He and Batman stormed the mayor's office and captured the Joker and Harley Quinn. They emerged into a cheering crowd as Superman flew onto the scene.

"Great job, Batman, Cyborg," Superman said. "Justice has been restored to Gotham City!"

"And now you guys can go back to wherever it is you hang out," Batman said.

"I can't leave your side, Batman," Cyborg said. "I saved your life. We're bonded, bro."

Batman groaned.

THE END

CONTINUED FROM PAGE 108.

Batman and Batgirl dodged left. The freeze blast missed them.

Batman moved quickly. His BatRope whipped out, wrapping around the blaster and tearing it out of Mr. Freeze's hands. Then he and Barbara ran past Mr. Freeze into the waterworks.

Massive water tanks towered overhead, and metal pipes snaked around the facility. They didn't get far when they heard the Penguin's voice overhead.

"Do you have my money, Batman?" the Penguin asked. "And who's that with you?"

"Oh, don't mind her," Batman replied. "And no, I don't have your money. Only justice."

"Excuse me?" Barbara exclaimed.

The Penguin scowled. "You're making a mistake, Batman," he said. "Penguins! Get them!"

Hundreds of the Penguin's minions appeared around them, waddling across the floor. The little robotic penguins wore red radio-controlled helmets so that the Penguin could give them commands. And each one held a tiny harpoon shooter.

"Fire!" the Penguin yelled.

As quick as a flash, Batman tossed a grappling hook attached to a strong line to one of the pipes overhead. He grabbed Barbara and they both swung up to the pipe, dodging the tiny harpoons.

Batman looked at his communicator. A tiny red dot blinked on the screen.

"I have a tracer on Alfred," he told Barbara. "He's somewhere under the facility."

"Why do you have a tracer on Alfred?" Barbara asked.

"That's not important," Batman replied.

With one arm around Barbara, he swung from pipe to pipe, following the tracer. Finally, he stopped in front of the Gotham City reservoir. Its waters fed the Gotham water supply.

"He's down there somewhere," Batman said.

Barbara looked down. "How will we get to him?"

"I've got this," Batman said. He pressed a button on his wrist communicator. Seconds later, a sleek black craft rose up from beneath the water. Batman hopped inside, and Barbara did the same.

Then Batman closed the clear bubble over the cockpit.

"Bat-Sub, descend!" Batman commanded.

The submarine slowly lowered into the water. The water was clear, but dark. Lights from the sub illuminated the path in front as Batman slowly steered through the water.

"I see something!" Barbara said.

The light shone on a clear cube completely submerged in the water. Two large tubes snaked out from the sides of the cube. There was no water inside the cube – but Alfred was there!

"Alfred!" Batman cried, but he knew that Alfred couldn't hear him.

"I see some kind of gears on the side of the cube," Barbara said, pointing. "Maybe there's a way to get Alfred out safely."

"Forget gears," Batman said. "I can just blast this baby wide open."

"No!" Barbara cried. "Alfred could get hurt!"

Batman grunted.

"I think those gears—" Barbara began.

"They open the tubes," Batman said. "Both of those tubes lead to the surface."

"Exactly," Barbara said. "But why are there two tubes? Where do they lead?"

Batman studied the gears. There were two gears – one large, and one small – with a handle on them.

"What does it matter?" Batman asked. "I just want to get Alfred out of there."

IF BATMAN TURNS THE BIG GEAR, GO TO PAGE 98.

IF BATMAN TURNS THE SMALL GEAR, GO TO PAGE 21.

CONTINUED FROM PAGE 141.

Batman jumped to the right to avoid Catwoman. His feet landed on soft grass. He turned to see a large, furry sloth lazing in a tree. Batman used the tree to swing back up onto the wall.

He caught up to Catwoman just as she jumped off the edge of the wall into a courtyard in the zoo. She ran to the Snack Shack, a small building with a peaked roof. A digital screen announced: TREATS FOR HUNGRY CITIZENS! She climbed up to the top of the roof with amazing agility.

Batman launched his grappling hook at the Snack Shack sign. It wrapped around the sign and he used the rope to swing himself up.

"You're no match for me on the rooftop, Batman," Catwoman taunted. "I'm a cat, and cats can balance anywhere."

"And I'm a bat, and bats can fly," Batman said.

He jumped up, grabbed a surprised Catwoman, and then launched off the rooftop. His cape billowed out behind him as he safely floated to the ground. Then he quickly snapped bat-shaped handcuffs onto Catwoman's wrists.

Alfred ran up.

"I've rounded up all the big cats!" he reported. "A little trick I learned while serving in the jungle. I made a noise like a wounded animal and lured them all into a pen."

"What is Bruce Wayne's butler doing here?" Catwoman asked.

"That's not important," Batman said. "What's important is that you're going to Arkham Asylum."

Catwoman rolled her eyes. "Ooh, I'm scared. It's not like I haven't escaped from there a million times before."

Batman knew she was right. But that's how it was in Gotham City. He captured villains. They got locked up in Arkham Asylum. Then they escaped and the cycle started all over again.

"You got any better ideas?" Batman asked.

"As a matter of fact, I do," Catwoman said. "I'm not a big fan of this Rogue City thing. I never wanted to be in charge of the zoo. I liked Gotham City better when I could steal things in the shadows and then go home and take care of my cats."

"That's not an idea," Batman pointed out.

"I'm getting to it," Catwoman replied. "Why don't you let me help you take down the Joker? I can help you – if you let me go."

Before Batman could answer, the digital screen

in the Snack Shack flickered. The Joker's face appeared.

"Attention, citizens of Gotham City!" he announced. "I have captured Superman! Super Heroes, surrender to me immediately!"

IF BATMAN LETS CATWOMAN HELP HIM STOP THE JOKER, GO TO PAGE 18.

IF BATMAN BRINGS CATWOMAN TO ARKHAM ASYLUM, GO TO PAGE 94.

CONTINUED FROM PAGE 67.

Where to start first? Batman wondered. *The botanical gardens? The waterworks? The zoo?*

Then it hit him: Once he started capturing Rogues, he needed somewhere to put them. And there was only one place in Gotham fit for the city's worst evildoers.

Arkham Asylum.

Batman headed north and quickly reached the tall walls that surrounded Arkham. The large brick buildings behind the gates, with their sloped roofs and dark windows, looked more like a compound of haunted houses than a hospital. Dark clouds hung in the sky over Arkham, but nowhere else in the city.

Batman parked the Batmobile out of sight and stealthily made his way to the fence. The Joker had said that he'd put Scarecrow in charge.

I've got to take out Scarecrow first, Batman thought. *Then I can take back the asylum.*

Any other hero might have shivered at the thought of facing the Scarecrow. Formerly known as Professor Jonathan Crane, the Scarecrow was an expert in fear. Just looking at him was enough to give you the heebie-jeebies. He looked like a living scarecrow, with raggedy clothes, a floppy hat, and red glowing eyes on his face.

Batman wasn't afraid. He produced a bat-shaped grappling hook attached to a strong line and tossed it up to the top of the fence, in a shadowy spot on the side of the building. He rappelled up the side of the wall. Just as he was about to drop down onto the ground, something hissed from the pointy tops of the fence. A green gas shot into the air.

Fear gas! Batman realized, and it was all around him. Before he could breathe it in, he felt someone pull on his legs. He fell to the ground, outside the fence, with a thud.

"What the—?" Batman spun around and saw Barbara Gordon getting to her feet.

"Sorry, Batman," she said. "I had to get you out of the way before you breathed in that Fear Gas."

"I was about to jump," Batman said.

Barbara frowned. "You're welcome."

"What are you doing here, anyway?" Batman asked.

"You can't take on these Rogues by yourself," Barbara said. "I told you, this is personal. I'm going to help you until we save the city and rescue my father."

Batman gazed up at the fence. "Looks like he's booby-trapped the whole fence. We should take the Batcopter up to the roof."

"There's an underground delivery entrance," Barbara said. "The Batcopter might attract too much attention."

"It's a stealth copter," Batman argued. "You know what stealth means, right?"

Barbara sighed. "Your choice, Batman."

IF BATMAN AND BARBARA TRY THE UNDERGROUND ENTRANCE, GO TO PAGE 156.

IF THEY TAKE THE BATCOPTER TO THE ROOF, GO TO PAGE 76.